AWAKENING

BOOK ONE OF THE EMBLEM AND THE LANTERN

DYLAN HIGGINS

Addie,
let the Light
of Christ
Shine in you!

Second Edition: Hill Harow Books: September 2011
Fourth Printing

Library of Congress Cataloging-in-Publication Data

Dylan Higgins.
        Awakening: Book One of The Emblem & The Lantern / by
Dylan Higgins; Illustrated by Mikael Jury.
    2nd ed.
    ISBN 13: 978-0615534398 (Hill Harow Books)
    ISBN 10: 0615534392
    This is a work of literary fiction.
            Edited by Susan Clough, Joanna Jury, Barbara Toth
                The text was set in Palatino.

This book is dedicated to my children who are meant for amazing things!

"Wake up, O sleeper, rise from the dead, and Christ will shine on you." (Ephesians 5:14)

CONTENTS

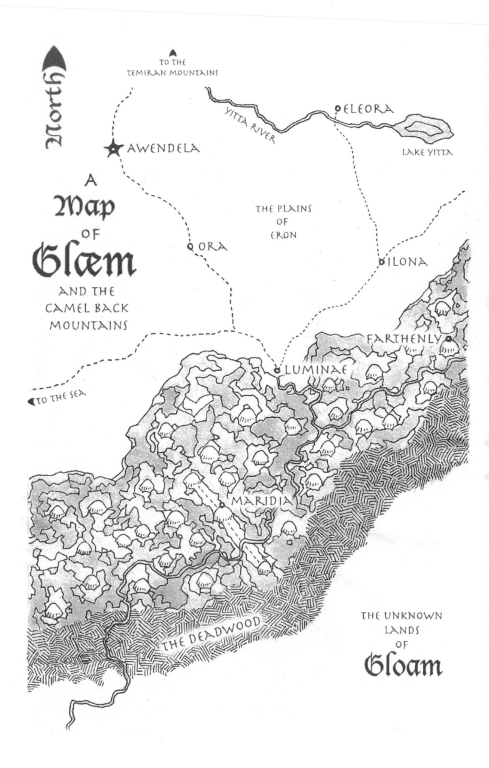

North

TO THE
TEMIRAN MOUNTAINS

YITTA RIVER

ELEORA

LAKE YITTA

A
Map
OF
Glæm
AND THE
CAMEL BACK
MOUNTAINS

AWENDELA

ORA

THE PLAINS
OF
ERON

ILONA

FARTHENLY

LUMINAE

TO THE SEA

MARIDIA

THE DEADWOOD

THE UNKNOWN
LANDS
OF
Gloam

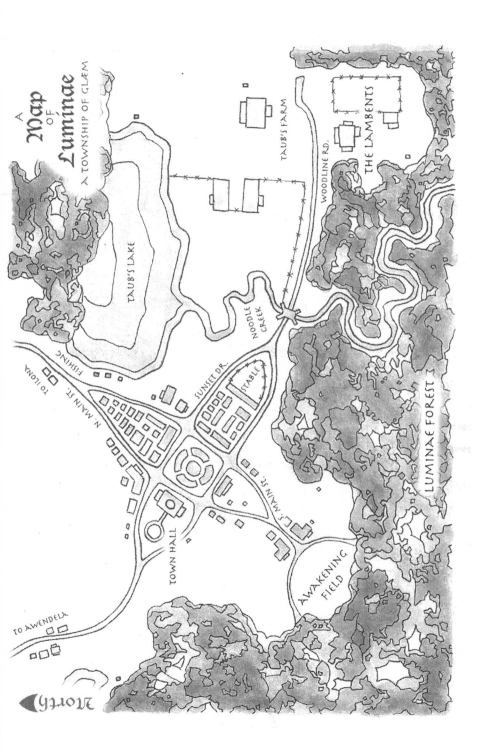

A Map OF Luminae
A TOWNSHIP OF GLÆM

North

TO AWENDELA

N. MAIN ST.

TO ILONA

FISHING

TAUB'S LAKE

TAUB'S FARM

WOODLINE RD.

THE LAMBENTS

NOODLE CREEK

SUNSET DR.

STABLE

S. MAIN ST.

TOWN HALL

AWAKENING FIELD

LUMINAE FOREST

Prologue

An ancient creature sleeps. It dreams of a light that grows bigger and bigger. The light burns and wakes the monster but only briefly for it finds itself safe, surrounded by absolute darkness. The ancient one falls back into its long and lightless slumber.

Chapter One
The Boy of Legend

This is a story of two lands and two young siblings. The lands spoken of herein are Glæm, a country of undying light and Gloam, a dominion of utter darkness. The origins of these lands are not recorded on the pages of this narrative – that is, in fact, an untold story. The children in this remarkable tale are Ethan and his sister Eisley. More directly, this is the account of Ethan and Eisley Lambent's unique and, it should be noted, spectacular journey into adulthood. The story begins in a small house on the edge of a large forest. The sun has set, yet darkness never completely falls. A chill in the air begins to wax as the Lambent family gathers in their home for a very special purpose. A cozy fire warms the sitting room and all eyes are upon a grandmotherly woman who is telling an ancient tale.

Her story is about a boy who lived on the edge of the forest in a village known as Luminae. In that age, Luminae was rather small and the townsfolk didn't wander very far into the trees that lay in shadow. Why would they? Life for those in Luminae (and for all Glæmians) was peaceful, and to disturb that peace with thoughts of wandering outside the safety of Glæm's borders was unheard of. Unheard of to all except the boy in the old woman's tale. Riley, as the boy was named, always thought it odd that no one in his bright world questioned what lay beyond Glæm.

On the night that Riley turned thirteen he decided to leave the comfort of his quaint village and travel into the Camel Back Mountains, which rise up from the heart of the forest. The boy's parents awoke the next morning to find their son missing. With help from the villagers, Riley's distraught mother and father searched for him for weeks, but to no avail. It was soon determined that he had either run away or had been taken. News of Riley's disappearance traveled quickly across the land, and before long every household in Glæm had heard of the boy. It greatly disturbed the Glæmians, for no one had ever gone missing in their country. Until now, Glæmian life had been peaceful and uneventful – at least in all of recorded history.

Seven years passed and one day the boy, now a man, returned to Luminae. With him were others. Scores of people with skin as pale as snow came out of the mountains and descended on Luminae. It is said that the most peculiar scene met those who lived closest to the forest and mountains: those who saw it said it looked as if the snow left the peaks and crept down from the mountains to pay the town a visit. The people of Luminae were frightened. They called their Elders into the streets to face the oncoming human blizzard. As Riley entered the town, news of his return began to spread. After a wonderful reunion with his parents, the young man shared the identity of the pale visitors. He told of a land beyond the Camel Back Mountains shrouded in eternal darkness by a vile creature named Smarr. The Gloamers, as they called themselves, were subject to the dark and had never seen nor heard of light in all their years. In fact, they hadn't a name for the darkness because there had never been anything to compare it to. Riley went on to tell of the Gloamer's strange reaction to the lantern he'd carried along. This Magic Lantern, as the Gloamers called it, was the very reason they decided to travel back to Glæm with Riley. They wanted to *see* more. They wanted to live in the light.

It is said that Riley, The Boy of Legend, told stories of Gloam's culture as well but these accounts have since been lost. What has lasted is the tradition of the Awakening – at the age of thirteen Glæm's young ones travel, by lantern light, into Luminae Forest and return the following day to be welcomed back as adults. Glæmians leave childhood at the same time the young man did.

The old storyteller gave a warm smile to the hearers of her tale.

"Now, Ethan and Eisley, it is your turn to participate in the Awakening."

Ethan Lambent was well aware of this. It had been the only thing on his mind in recent weeks. His twin sister, Eisley, hadn't given much thought to the Awakening because she wasn't as ready to grow up as her brother. Looking at his sister, Ethan could tell that their grandmother's story, a Glæmian favorite heard so many times before, had not captivated her like it had him. Eisley sat on the glowing hearth, fiddling with the fire poker, prodding the embers. Even if his sister wasn't looking forward to adulthood, Ethan was. So he listened to the old tale with new zeal. Ethan had been preparing for continued studies throughout Glæm and coming of age would accelerate his plans. His favorite pastime was digging deep into books, though Eisley cared little for further study. She felt that she'd had enough of schooling but, to oblige her parents, she'd continue down the same academic road as her brother. Eisley was as intelligent as Ethan yet, lacked interest in formal education. Eisley was more inclined to focus on her physical abilities. She was a very fast runner, so fast that she'd made a name for herself in town being the only girl who could outrun the boys. In addition to her speed Eisley could climb like a spider, very much unlike her brother who didn't see the point in such things.

Being twins, Ethan and Eisley shared many of the same features. Both had dark brown hair; Ethan's was straight, Eisley's a bit wavy. The two had bright blue eyes, fair complexions and stood near the same height, tall for their age. Of course Ethan had certain boyish qualities that contrasted with Eisley's more girlish ones. While similar in appearance a deeper comparison of the twins would reveal many differences. For instance, in decision-making, Ethan was very calculated, taking hours and sometimes days to come to a conclusion. Eisley only took moments to make up her mind because she thought with her heart rather than her head. Ethan had an intense nature, being totally focused on his interests, which were many. He was always planning for a bigger, better future. Eisley was laid back, taking each day as it came and being generally content with life as it was. All in all, the two had polar opposite personalities.

Ethan looked at his grandmother, Jaine Lambent, watching her as she spoke, paying close attention to the way the fire cast shadows across her face. Jaine was the family storyteller and the twins had heard her tell *The Tale of the Boy of Legend* many times before and the story had ended just as it always had – but not this time. Nothing could have prepared the twins for what their grandmother would say next. Jaine let out a long sigh, looking at her husband, Emmett as she did so. Then Jaine eyed the twin's parents, Amory and Evangeline, as if seeking some sort of approval. Amory and Evangeline nodded, and Jaine began. "My dear grandchildren, as you know, all the children of Glæm have heard this story. Most Glæmians believe that the Boy of Legend is nothing more than legend. Yet he was so much more. Riley actually lived."

Ethan and Eisley regarded one another with curiosity.

"Riley *Lambent* was as real as anyone in this room."

First surprise, and then comprehension spread across the twins' faces.

"Riley *Lambent*? He's related to us?" asked Eisley.

"Yes," Jaine replied, "He was."

"But that's ridiculous, he's only a faerie tale," said Ethan.

The twins turned toward their parents as if looking for grins that would end this ridiculous charade. However, none came.

"This is not a joke," said Amory, "Your grandmother is telling the truth."

Their mother nodded in confirmation.

Everyone in Glæm knew of Riley yet he'd never had a surname in the tales. Could this really be true?

"I don't understand," said Ethan. "Why haven't we been told before? Why does no one else know the boy's surname?"

"This secret's been long kept by the Lambent family," said Grandpa Emmett.

"But why?" asked Ethan.

"The answer is simple," replied their grandmother. "But first, let me address why we are only telling you just now. In the past, there have been those in our family who decided to tell their children when they were younger than you. The children became obsessed with the heroic acts of their ancestor and decided to follow in his path... a dangerous thing for a child to do. This happened to Earnest Lambent. I'm sure you've heard his name before."

The two nodded. Earnest traveled into the Camel Back Mountains never to be heard from again.

"Earnest's disappearance led newer generations to tell their children at the Awakening... as adults."

"Which you two are becoming," added Evangeline.

"Yes," agreed Jaine. "We can only hope that neither of you will become quite as adventurous as some of the Lambents of the past."

"Then why even tell us at all?" asked Eisley, "I mean, why does it even matter?"

"Because, dear, it is your right as Lambents to know the truth of our family history."

"As to your question of why the rest of Glæm doesn't know, I offer this answer," said Jaine.

At that moment Jaine reached around and uncovered an object beneath a tattered piece of cloth, lying on the kitchen table. Ethan had noticed the oddly-shaped bundle when Jaine placed it there earlier. Grandma Jaine turned, holding an old lantern. Its appearance wasn't much. The brass lantern was a foot high and bore many dents and scuffs along the outer frame that held the glass center. Smaller crisscrossing wires actually held the glass interior snug in its place. The only other noticeable feature was a thin, rounded handle fixed to the top. An uncomfortable silence gripped the room that was only broken by the crackling of the fire. Ethan stood up and approached the lantern. He started to understand how significant the object was that he now studied.

"Is…" attempted Ethan, unable to form a sentence.

"Yes," said Jaine, "this is the very same lantern that Riley Lambent took into the land of Gloam. The Magic Lantern."

Eisley now stood inches behind Ethan. Brother and sister examined the lantern in wonder.

"Do we get to use it at our Awakening?" asked Eisley.

"Yes, Eisley Girl," answered her father. "In two days you will take it with you into the forest for the night."

"If the town elders knew you had this…they would –" began Ethan.

"They'd snatch it from us and bury it in a museum in the Shinin' City!" finished Emmett.

"And we revere this heirloom too much to see it taken from our care. Chances are, we would never get it back, losing a precious piece of our heritage," said Jaine.

Ethan agreed. He knew that if the lantern was discovered it would end up in the shining city of Awendela, the capital of Glæm, which stood far and away to the northwest.

"Besides," continued Jaine, "it is of much more value to our family because it is not actually magical as the story implies…"

"Not magical?" said Emmett under his breath.

"THE GLOAMERS HAD, simply, never *seen* anything before this lantern brought light to them and they were naturally drawn to it," said Jaine trying to drown out Emmett's comment but failing.

Talk of a magic lights reminded Ethan of an old saying, that in complete darkness a Glæmian would shine as if the light of the sun was actually radiating through them. This had never truly been tested to Ethan's knowledge. And how could it? The sky carried some form of light at all times. Glæm had a sun by day and three moons by night. On any given night at least two of the Brother Moons shone in the sky. Sometimes all three of the brothers were out, depending upon their placement in the heavens. (Perhaps you are wondering at this very moment whether there were any caves or maybe even rooms without windows in the land of Glæm. Well, windowless rooms did not exist in this land, what an absurd invention that would be. As for the caves…surely there were caves, but no one cared enough about finding such dark places to even test this theory of 'glowing Glæmians'. Why would anyone want to wade in the darkness when they had refreshing, amazing, all encompassing, never-ending light?)

Ethan made a mental note to do further studies of this *internal glow* notion. But at the moment, Emmett's curious comment aside, Ethan thought that the lantern probably wasn't magical. If light actually lived inside Glæmians to such an extent that it shone through, what use would a lantern be to them?

"I understand why we would want to keep the lantern in our family, but how in all of Glæm did the Lambents hide the boy's last name?" asked Eisley.

"Fortunately this was easier to deal with than the other matter," answered Emmett, "time's been a friend to the Lambent family."

The twins looked confounded.

"Truth is, over time our people forgot Riley's proper name," clarified Emmett.

"Isn't it funny how if we or our parents or even our parents' parents aren't personal witnesses to something, we begin to doubt the truth of it? Things so easily become myth," added Amory.

"And so it is with *this* truth," said Evangeline.

Then Eisley asked, "Can no one else know about this? Not even friends? Its seems a shame to have such an interesting family history and not be able to tell others."

"No, dear, no one else can know. We have kept this secret for a long time," answered Grandma Jaine.

"I know the two of you have been given a lot to think about tonight and need time to ponder it, so you should probably head off to bed," said Amory.

"And we should probably get home ourselves," said Grandpa Emmett.

Ethan and Eisley, minds reeling, got up to hug their grandparents before heading to their rooms. "Hey," voiced their mother. "Don't think you're getting out of kitchen duty. If the cook has to clean then so do you!" The twins groaned all the way to the kitchen.

While cleaning up after a festive dinner of roasted turkey and an assortment of breads and cheeses, Ethan began to think about the meal and why they'd had it in the first place. This was a special dinner they had every year at this time. It was customary for all of Glæm to celebrate the Awakening once a year with feasts and fellowship. It just so happened that the Lambent twins' birthday fell on the exact same day as the annual Awakening celebration. As such, there were more people in town than normal visiting for the special occasion, which led Ethan to think of their other grandparents, Charston and Noemi Hale, who were missing for the first time from this event. He wondered whether or not they had been asked to stay home because of the telling of this Lambent family secret. And then turning to his mother to voice this assumption, he asked, "Do your parents know about Riley Lambent?"

"Sadly, they do not," answered Evangeline. "And they cannot know. I'm only allowed to know because I married your father."

Eisley stood at the sink, listening to the conversation between her mother and brother. "It must be hard keeping such a thing from your parents, huh?"

"It really is; though, I have found it much harder keeping it from the two of you." She smiled. "I'm sure you can see, from the Lambent family's dreadful history in misusing this secret, why we waited until you were more mature before telling you," said Evangeline. "I couldn't bare to loose either one of you to the darkness." She almost whispered.

The moment broke as the children began to laugh at the idea of brother and sister taking off into the mountains towards the unknown lands beyond. It sounded so absurd and their laughter seemed to comfort their mother. Yet, in secret, Ethan knew that his mother's worry wasn't completely unwarranted.

Later that night, while lying in bed, the boy who was soon to be a man stared out the window toward the two moons that shone like eyes in the night sky. While his family slept and dreamt, Ethan lay awake far into the night. His thoughts were elsewhere. Perhaps as far as a land called Gloam.

Chapter Two

The Awakening

The next day buzzed with preparations for the Awakening ceremony, set to begin the following evening. Grandpa Charston and Grandma Noemi arrived early that morning. They didn't seem too upset about missing the traditional family feast the night before. In fact, Charston, along with Emmett and Amory, left the house before sun up to scout out a safe place for Eisley and Ethan to camp during their Awakening ceremony. Ethan begged to go along with them. But his mother firmly denied his request for reasons she kept to herself. So for Ethan the greater part of the day was spent setting up the tent to make sure that it was in proper working order and traversing the cluttered attic to find the camping essentials: sleeping sacks, carryalls, water flasks, and a knife. The lighting for the trip was taken care of years in advance, of course.

Ethan appeared cheerful to the others throughout the day, but secretly he felt ill at ease since the moment Riley Lambent's name had been revealed. He began to dream of leaving Glæm, yet he knew how absurd those thoughts were. He even went so far as to try talking *to* himself saying things like, "You can't seriously be planning such naive things." Or, "What would your parents and sister do if you never came back?"

He finally subdued the audible exchange with himself when his one and only neighbor, Mr. Taubs, overheard a bit of his conversation from across the road. He shrugged it off and asked Mr. Taubs to come over and help him put the tent together. The old man obliged Ethan's request for help, assuming that the boy had been reading aloud the instructions on tent assembly. Ethan hoped Mr. Taubs would think something of the sort. It wouldn't be good to build a reputation as someone who talks aloud to himself.

Try as he might, Ethan couldn't shake the burgeoning desire to follow in his ancestor's footsteps. He agreed with Riley's stance on the overly content state of Glæmians, and pondered why Riley's curiosity and travels had never spurred similar adventures from others like himself, even if he had only been a myth to his people. Were Glæmians really so satisfied in their bright existence as to never allow curiosity to drive them to explore a land outside of their own? Was *his* family so satisfied? Furthermore, with the possible existence of Gloamers living in perpetual darkness, how could *no one* have gone in search of them?

Ethan's thoughts fueled the growing fire in his mind. Soon he had completely talked himself into leaving Glæm under the pretense of aiding Gloamers. But, truth be told, he had simply discovered adventure in his blood. In less than a day, he went from looking forward to a future as a scholar of the lands of enduring light to a state of total discontent.

Eisley's morning hadn't been much different from her brother's. She spent her time organizing the things that Ethan retrieved from the attic. She unrolled and re-rolled the sleeping sacks, filled the water flasks, sharpened the knife, then fit them all perfectly into the carryalls. She, along with the other women in her family, spent most of the forenoon in the kitchen, baking bread for the journey. The warm, fresh bread was to be an addition to the leftovers that Evangeline had scrounged together from the Awakening feast the night before. The twins' mother complained about having no green vegetables to send along with the meal, but she did manage to include a few apples, which made her feel a little better.

Eisley finished all the packing for their journey by lunchtime, including the food. While she worked, Eisley let her mind wander. She began to think about what the first year of adulthood would be like, and was surprised that these thoughts brought with them a tinge of anxiety. Rather than eat lunch, she decided to do what she had always done when feeling nervous. She decided to run.

Eisley had been running since the time she was old enough to walk. In her mind's eye, the streets of Luminae wound together as jogging routes, not simply roads. Through her young eyes, nothing had ever really changed in the old town. The Lambents lived in the house closest to the Luminae Forest and farthest from the center of town making it a fair distance to run. There were not many neighbors on the southern leg of Woodline Road, where the Lambents' home sat snug in the outlying trees. Only one other home-place was located directly across the road occupied by a longtime resident of Luminae, Mr. Taubs.

Mr. Taubs was a kind old man whose face crinkled into a smile when he saw Eisley turn out of her drive and head toward town. Mr. Taubs had more land in the town than anyone else. He owned Taubs' Farm, which spanned over three hundred acres of fences and farm animals. Mr. Taubs also had somewhat of a monopoly in Luminae on products like meat and dairy. But no one seemed to mind because he was so generous, allowing the townsfolk, and particularly the men, access to his hundred-acre lake that nestled against the northern boundary of his property. Taubs' Lake, as it was called, housed the biggest fish in all of southern Glæm. In the warmer seasons the people of Luminae could keep their bellies full of fish without losing an ounce from their money purses.

"All in all," thought Eisley, as she began her run, "you couldn't ask for a better neighbor."

Eisley's jog took her, as usual, up Woodline Road into the center of town, where the meeting hall rose above the trees on the far side of the square. Town Hall was built rather elaborately because it was the first building travelers would see as they came in on the road from the Shining City. This public building was three-stories high and made of brick, which was rare in southern Glæm. The top of the town hall was a brass dome that looked out of place in comparison to the rest of the town's wood and stone structures. As Eisley neared the hub of Luminae she noticed that performance stages were set up in the middle of the typically empty square. Festivities always accompanied the Awakening's annual celebration. The entertainment included local music (of which her father was sometimes a part of), dancing and poetry reading along with cart-loads of food. As Eisley passed, the stages stood abandoned, looking a bit lonely by her reckoning.

Eisley afforded a quick glance to her left down South Main Street, which ran directly into Luminae Forest at the far end. It was on this stretch of road that all the inns stood ready to house the steady stream of out-of-towners who flooded Luminae year round. Visitors came from all over Glæm to attend their own families' Awakening ceremonies. Shops lined the streets on this same stretch of road dealing in various Awakening memorabilia and supplies. Selling wooden plaques and scrolls that gave a personal account of an individual's awakening had become quite a booming enterprise.

Yet to Eisley and to most locals, this street was avoided at all costs. The town's officials did their best to prevent this ordinarily congested area from spilling over into the rest of Luminae. In fact, in all her life, her family had only been to Awakening Field once to commemorate a close friend's rite of passage. The field that was used for "farewells" and "welcome backs" during the Awakening was a large semi-circle. The forest bordered the far end of the field while the street bound the other edge. Eisley could barely see Awakening Field from her position near the center of town.

As she turned, heading northeast up Main Street, she thought of how her family had decided to hold her and Ethan's ceremony in their own back yard rather than mix with the outside crowd. Eisley was perfectly fine with this arrangement, not caring much for crowds – a trait she'd inherited from her mother. It actually made the whole ordeal a little less painful and more meaningful. She turned right and ran down Sunset Drive, a small side lane that led her past the stables where visitors usually housed their mounts. This street wound back into Woodline Road, to complete her loop and set her on a course for home.

Feeling less anxious than before, Eisley returned home. She entered the kitchen to find that the apples had been removed from Ethan's pack. Wondering at this she opened her bother's carryall to investigate. Inside she discovered quite a mess; the bag was crammed full of much more than when she had packed it. With a sigh Eisley began to pack the bag, again. To her surprise, Ethan stuffed the carrier full with other items: a jar of nuts, a bag of berries and strips of cured meat. In the very bottom of the carryall, Eisley found…a few extra changes of clothes. Did he plan to stay in the forest more than just one night? The answer was yes. She knew now that the story of Riley Lambent had stirred him just like it had stirred previous generations of Lambents.

The rest of the day, Eisley said nothing to Ethan of her discovery, nor did she speak a word to their parents. Though she was not enthusiastic about going any further into the forest than needed, Eisley would follow her brother because she loved him. She could not stand to think of him being hurt or lost without being there by his side. Still, deep down she too began to think of Riley Lambent's journey. Without even noticing the change, a yearning for the unknown took hold of her as it had her brother.

That night around the dinner table Ethan wore a somber expression on his face.

"What's the matter son?" asked Amory.

Ethan looked up from his untouched food to respond, "Uh...nothing really. I've...just got a lot on my mind at the moment. That's all."

"That's understandable. Have you decided where you'd liked to begin studying after the Awakening?"

"Yeah, I've been thinking of going to Awendela first," said Ethan, noticing a sideways glance from his sister.

"All the way to the Shining City?" asked Evangeline. "Wouldn't you like to start somewhere a bit...closer?" she asked.

"Um...yeah, I'll think about it," Ethan answered as he prodded at his food.

"Are you sure you're all right?" asked Amory, unrelenting.

"Yeah...positive."

Really, Ethan wasn't all right. He started to treat every waking moment in his house, with his family, as the very last. His senses were more acute than normal as he took in his surroundings: the kitchen table with its rounded edges and, as he noticed for the first time, many scratches and dings from what looked like hundreds of knife marks left from years of food preparation. There was also a distinct smell to this house that he'd never really noticed before: a mixture of oak, cedar and stone. He tried his hardest to catalogue the smell in his memory so that he would never forget it. The ceilings were lower than he remembered, or maybe he was just taller than the last time he'd actually noticed. Come to think of it, the whole house was a bit smaller than he'd ever recalled. What an odd thing to have always lived in this house and only now, at what might be the end, really notice it for the first time. And then there was his family. His mother, with her long chestnut hair, was in her early thirties although she didn't look a day older than twenty. Time has been good to her. To her left sat his father, the man he hoped he'd be like someday. If that day ever came. Amory had dark hair just like Evangeline with more gray highlights than Ethan remembered. His father wore a big bushy beard all year round, which was kept at the request of his mother. Ethan thought that he might actually look similar to his father – if he could grow a beard. Lastly, Eisley sat between himself and his mother. She had long wavy brown hair that fell into curly locks at the end. Her fair skin and rosy cheeks were a wonderful complement to her bright blue eyes, which she could use to speak with just as easily as her voice. One always knew Eisley's state of mind simply by looking into her eyes. Ethan felt a pang of regret at the thought of leaving his twin behind, the one he'd grown up with, discovered life with. How would he be able to leave her? He knew nothing of life without his twin, and his leaving would tear her apart. Eisley seemed to bare the same expression as he, which Ethan thought odd. Here they were, together in their home for what might be the last time. Though he was saddened by this notion, it did not lessen his resolve in the slightest. He knew what he had to do. He knew like he'd never known anything before. It was as if some outside force was driving him into a dark and unfamiliar place.

Ethan slept soundly that last night at home, much to his relief. He fell asleep thinking of how much he loved his life and his family. Ethan understood a little easier now why no one had ever left Glæm. It was such a lovely place. But lovely or not, it was time to go.

The twins had a fairly idle day, as all the preparation had been seen to the morning before. As such, they spent time with their family, gathered around the fire, recalling memories of the twins' earlier years. Each grandparent had a favorite memory of times spent with their grandchildren. More often than not, Ethan and Eisley were so young during the actual occurrence of those recollections that they barely even remembered them happening at all.

What they did remember clearly were their parents' stories, for these memories were some of the twins' fondest as well. Amory told stories about their many adventures wandering through the edge of the forest. Ethan remembered the time that he and his father had spent there, building huts and sometimes just walking together. Their mother was fond of their weekly trips to the town library. She was sure that they'd read every book available in Luminae. Though, the library wasn't very large, and neither was the book selection.

One of the most favorite memories that both Ethan and Eisley shared with their parents was the numerous nights spent around the fire singing songs and dancing together.

Their father always loved writing and singing songs. He also loved playing the kithara: a plucked stringed instrument with a long neck bearing frets and a rounded body with a flat front shaped like a halved egg. The songs and dances would stretch far into the wee hours of the lesser light on many occasions. Amory wrote hymns about the Creator, life and love.

The previous day, during the men's hunt for a good camping spot, Amory conveniently stumbled upon a snug little clearing about two miles into the forest. Charston said the clearing was hard to see into because of the undergrowth surrounding it, making it a bit safer for the twins. Ethan thought that the underbrush would make it hard to see out of as well and this news might complicate his departure plans if there were relatives keeping a concealed eye-out for himself and his sister during the night.

Ethan had to devise a way to explain to Eisley what he was planning to do. He decided that he would tell her over dinner in the clearing, when they were finally alone.

The early afternoon crept on and the time came for the twins to make their move into the new world of adulthood. There were hugs and kisses all around and the women were teary-eyed, as was Amory, which came as no surprise.

"Your father is a lover not a fighter," Evangeline told the children once, though one day this statement would not be entirely true.

After saying their goodbyes Ethan and Eisley were given a small map to their destination. The hand-drawn map displayed the tip of the forest that wrapped around the rear of the Lambent's property. In the bottom left corner there was a clearing with only few icons sketched between it and the edge of the wood. The twins would have to pass over Noodle Creek, named that for its squiggly shape. Noodle Creek sprung from Mr. Taub's lake, and ran deep into the forest. No Glæmian knew just how far away the creek flowed. Next they would have to turn due west at Stepping Stone, a large rock that jutted up out of the top of the canopy of trees. Staying this course would lead them directly to the glade chosen by their elders. They began to walk and as they neared the woods, Ethan turned back to take one last, long look at the family and home he loved so much. Unnoticed by Ethan, Eisley did the same. With one last wave towards their family the twins slipped into Luminae Forest.

It didn't take long to make it to the clearing. As they approached the snug glade Ethan took note of just how hard it was to see into – or to get into for that matter. There were plenty of hiding places in which loved ones might check in on them over the course of their stay.

Eisley was thinking about the brush as well.

"Do you think they could have picked a safer clearing for us?" she laughed.

"Prison is more like it," said Ethan.

"I'm sure Mother and Father would prefer to think of it as fortress rather than a prison," said Eisley.

"Yeah...I suppose," replied Ethan as he removed his carryall from his back and dropped to the ground.

The siblings spent a good hour setting up camp. To their disbelief, a fire pit full of dry wood waited in the middle of the site upon their entering. All they could do was laugh. Their family did love them. There was no denying that fact.

As the sun began to drop behind the mountains, Ethan knew it was time to prepare their evening meal and tell his sister about his plans. He went into the tent and opened his carryall to retrieve the food. He was shocked to find that the contents of the bag had been rearranged and organized much more efficiently that when he had repacked them. Without a doubt, the organizational genius standing outside the tent had done this. Did that mean she already knew? Ethan dropped the bag and backed his way out of the tent. As he rose, he turned to face Eisley. There she stood with her pack fastened tightly to her back, holding in one hand the glowing lantern that had once belonged to Riley Lambent.

Chapter Three

No Regrets

The lantern in Eisley's hand shone brilliantly through the tiny clearing. The rays that shot forth from the depths of that ancient vessel seemed unnaturally far-reaching. Ordinarily, the light from a lamp such as this would glow evenly. It should have been brightest near the casing and dimmer as it stretched outward, but the luminescence from this particular lantern seemed to jet out in long rays that grew wider with their length. The rays of light moved about seemingly of their own accord, something like a prism refracting the light of the sun as it spins on string. Glæm's pale dusk dimmed the forest, and the Magic Lantern glowed even more mysteriously in the glade.

The spectacle of light dancing on the surrounding tree trunks distracted Ethan, and it took him a few moments to remember his reason for exiting the tent so quickly. Regaining his train of thought, Ethan said, "You already knew I was leaving."

"It didn't take too much to figure that out. As many times as you've asked me to pack for you, don't you think I'd notice when my work has been tampered with?"

Ethan hadn't seen this coming. Eisley's discovery of his plan had taken him off guard, and he wasn't sure what his next step would be. Surely, he couldn't follow through if his sister expected to go along. He had to keep her safe first and foremost.

"You *cannot* go, Eisley," said Ethan.

Eisley expected this reaction from him. "When I found the extra things shoved into your pack yesterday, I started watching you closely. There has been a change in you. You've always been determined, especially in your studies, but since Grandma Jaine told us about Riley Lambent there has been a more focused intent in you."

Ethan knew his sister was right. He had changed drastically in a matter of minutes after hearing the Boy of Legend's true identity. Ever since, he hadn't been able to think of anything but the unknown lands that lay beyond the borders of Glæm.

"You say that I *cannot* follow you, but I will. You can't stop me," said Eisley. "Besides, I'm faster than you."

Eisley had just shown a side of herself that Ethan had never seen before. There was so much resolve in her voice. Though she hadn't said it just then, Ethan knew now how much his sister loved him. In that moment, a bond formed between the twins like none before and possibly like would never be seen between any brother and sister anywhere. There was no use in arguing. Eisley had won.

"Ok. You can go," surrendered Ethan.

"Good," said Eisley, satisfied with the outcome of the talk.

"Do you have any plans beyond traipsing off in a Gloamward direction?" asked Eisley as she sat the lantern down on a tree stump next to her.

Her question brought an unsettling feeling to Ethan's gut. He had half-mindedly decided to go to Gloam to save its inhabitants from the darkness. Yet, as he now had to articulate this idea to his sister, it all sounded a bit far-fetched. How could he actually persuade any Gloamers to come back with him? He wasn't Riley Lambent. Ethan saw what he hadn't seen before – that what he wanted most was the journey itself. "Really, I had thought to set off into the mountains and see where they lead me." Ethan was embarrassed at the truth of this.

"I knew you had a curious mind," said Eisley, "but who knew of your adventurous spirit? It's not like you to do something without a good reason."

Eisley was pretty sure their ancestor hadn't known that Gloam existed when he first ventured there. She thought that he would have left Glæm with no clearer intentions than her brother now voiced. Adventure had seized them both across the centuries.

"Yeah," said Ethan, "Like you said, I've changed."

For once he was the one thinking more with his heart than his head. Had their personalities completely reversed at the mentioning of Riley Lambent and the lantern? No. Even in her decision to follow Ethan, Eisley let her heart lead her. She loved her brother and would follow him for that reason alone.

"So what now?" Eisley inquired. "Do we leave now or in the morning?"

"I don't know. I hadn't considered having you travel with me. I planned on leaving in the morning after helping you pack. I wanted to make sure you would be alright heading home alone."

The two decided to stick to Ethan's original plan and stay the night in the clearing, and leave at the first sign of dawn.

Morning came quickly. Tearing down the camp took the twins no time at all in their eagerness to begin their journey. They packed their carryalls and fastened the sleeping sacks underneath them. Ethan decided to bare the extra burden of the tent and found an efficient way to secure it to his bag. They put out the fire and stood, ready to leave.

Eisley looked concerned. Her eyes were downcast and Ethan noticed it.

"Are you sure about this, Eisley?"

"Yes, I'm positive," she replied, after a moment's thought. "Actually, I was just imagining Mother and Father's faces at the shock of finding our campsite empty."

"You won't have to worry about that sweetie," came a voice from behind the twins, "I'll make sure they know where yer off ta."

Ethan and Eisley jumped with surprise, both spinning toward the voice. It was Grandpa Emmett, standing there in his wrinkled clothes and long white hair looking rather disheveled. He appeared to be worn to a frazzle.

"Wha- what are you doing here, Grandpa?" Ethan's heart sank thinking his plan wouldn't work now.

"Well, surely you didn't think your mom and pop were gonna leave you out here all night without somebody keeping an eye on you? You otta know better than that."

Though he'd expected this of his parents, it still hurt Ethan's pride. Eisley didn't seem to mind the watchful eyes of their family, but she had realized, like Ethan, that their scheme was probably screeching to a halt. Before either grandson or granddaughter could get a word in edgewise, Emmett continued, "Don't bother trying to explain where yer off ta at such an early hour. I've been here the whole night."

Their grandfather knew *everything*. Ethan tried to speak but stuttered.

"Boy, don't even think about making up excuses now. 'Sides, it was already plain enough that you two were up to something from the way you've been acting the last coupla days."

Ethan lost himself, trying to think of ways to get around his grandfather.

"And don't think about trying to get by me either," said Emmett.

Had his grandfather read his mind? Ethan watched as his plans dissipated before his very eyes.

"Ya see, Ethan, yer parents suspected something like this might happen. Amory was supposed to be the one keeping an eye on the two of ya, but I persuaded him to let me do it instead."

"Why?" asked Ethan. "Why would you volunteer to stay in the wood if you didn't have to?"

"Well…that's a bit of a long story, son," answered Emmett with a yawn. Emmett had always called Ethan "son" and Ethan didn't mind at all. It somehow made him feel closer to his grandfather.

"Apparently we've got time now," responded Ethan.

"You have less time than ya think," said his grandfather, in such a way that heightened Ethan's curiosity and frustration.

"I don't understand," said Eisley.

Emmett looked back and forth between the twins. "What I am 'bout to do might be the biggest mistake of me life. It is very possible that yer parents did you wrong by allowing me to watch over you."

He paused.

"I'm not gonna stop you from leaving."

Uncertainty seized the twins. What was Grandpa Emmett saying?

Eisley watched as heavy tears formed in her beloved grandfather's eyes, which brought hot tears to her own eyes as well. "Why, Grandpa? *Why* are you letting us go?"

Emmett ignored her question for the moment. "First, we gotta get moving. Yer parents won't expect ya home until lunchtime, so you'll need the next few hours to get some distance 'tween you before they have all of Luminae searching on yer tails."

He led the way out of the clearing and headed south, deeper into the forest. Momentarily taken off guard by their grandfather's sudden departure, Ethan and Eisley regained their composure, quickly donned their packs and ran to catch up to him.

"Are you going with us, Grandpa?" Eisley questioned, hopefully.

"No, Eisley girl, I'm not. My time for travlin' has come and gone," said Emmett. "I'm going to tell you something that I haven't spoken of since, oh...before you were born. Like Earnest Lambent and Riley before him, I did some adventurin' of my own."

"When?" asked Ethan. The three pressed deeper into the wood, as into a dream.

"I was twenty years old," answered Emmett.

"Does the rest of the family know? Does grandma know?" said Ethan.

"Son," said Emmett with a chuckle, "your grandma came from the mountains. 'Course she knows and so does the rest of the family."

Ethan wondered if the surprises would ever end.

"Like the two of you, I wanted to follow in Riley's footsteps. I did some explorin' through the forest and mountains, journeyin' mostly in the region that lies to the north and east of here. I hardly had time to travel into the southern parts of the Camel Back Mountains, let alone make it all the way to Gloam. There is so much to see whichever way you go." He smiled to himself. "Anyway, I chose a northerly path, which led to a small settlement – Farthenly, as it is called, or was called. I'm not sure if it still exists. Farthenly sat on the top of one of the smaller mountains. I spied the small village through the trees as I was traveling, and decided to go there. I reached the settlement to be greeted by none other than yer grandmother," he paused as if remembering the moment and then began again.

"Jaine was down on her knees, working in a garden next to her house. I was afraid that I had startled her but rather than run, she slowly got to her feet and just stood there, staring at me. I couldn't take my eyes off of her." He sighed and remembered his audience. "I can't explain what happen to me that day, but in that very moment, I knew she belonged to me and I to her. My desire to adventure any further had gone away. I traded a *good* adventure for the *grandest* of 'em all."

Emmett paused long enough for Ethan to ask, "What? What was the grandest adventure?"

His grandfather only smiled before continuing his story.

"Even though my journey through the mountains ended in Farthenly, I can remember clearly the burning that I felt for the thrill of adventure. That's why I'm lettin' you go. I was the first since the ill-fated Earnest to go gallivantin' 'cross the hills, and I was also the last. 'Til the two of you, that is. Your father never felt the urge to venture down that same road." He looked at Eisley. "I must say I was a bit surprised when I heard that ya were going along with your brother. I almost changed my mind about the whole thing. But, I knew that even if I stopped ya today, you'd both find a way of escape soon enough." He shrugged. "So I decided to help ya."

Ethan frowned, unsatisfied. "You didn't answer my question, Grandpa. What was this grand adventure you mentioned?"

"You haven't figured it out yet, boy?" laughed Emmett. "*Love*, son. The greatest adventure is love."

Ethan disagreed, but decided now wasn't the time for arguing with his grandfather.

The travelers trekked for many hours, yet with Emmett telling stories from his own journey, time flew by. Her grandparents' love story captivated Eisley, and she wanted to hear more.

"Grandpa, what happened after you and grandma first met? Did her parents like you? Did you get to meet them?" In all her life Eisley had never heard Grandma Jaine speak of her parents.

Emmett answered, "No, child, yer great grand-parents passed away many years before I arrived in Farthenly. Jaine lived there with her father's brother and his family and she had no other relatives. So when I turned up there wasn't much fuss to be had over whether she should come back with me or not. Her family had lived in Farthenly for many generations and Glæm and Gloam were both foreign countries to them. But, unlike the Glæmians and Gloamers, the people of Farthenly had heard of both the land of light and the land of darkness. Funny things was, they chose to live between the two countries. The people of the village lived as self sufficiently as possible, but according to Jaine, they always struggled to provide for themselves. There were no other towns close enough to properly trade with. Rather than move to Glæm, they chose to live a half-life. Not a good sort of life to live, really."

"Were the people of Farthenly originally from Glæm or Gloam?" wondered Ethan.

"A good question, son," answered Emmett, "'Cordin' to Jaine, the Farthenly folk never kept any written records of themselves, which means we're not sure where they came from."

"What were they like Grandpa?" asked Eisley.

"Well, they were simple people whose lives where built around farming. There were no rulers of any sort. They were just ordinary farmers who lived as unselfishly as an individual can, outside the light of Glæm."

"Did anything exciting happen on your journey?" asked Ethan. "I mean, other than meeting grandma," he added quickly.

Emmett let out a great sigh. "No...there's really nothing left to tell of *my* story, but *yers* are just beginning. Such an exciting time this must be for the two of ya."

Their grandfather's smile nearly stretched from ear to ear. He seemed truly happy for them, although there was a touch of sadness in his eyes as well.

Ethan wondered what his grandpa would tell his mother and father but he couldn't bring himself to ask.

"The only other thing I can contribute to yer quest is a map I drew of the northern region of the mountains."

Emmett tugged an old, folded and worn piece of parchment from his pocket, the soft wrinkles hinting that this map had clearly seen many travels. Ethan knew he and Eisley were nearing the final moments of their grandpa's part in *their* story. ~~The boy~~ rather, the young man (for his Awakening Ceremony had passed with the rising of the sun), stood in awe of his grandfather. He could see how much it hurt Emmett to let them go alone. Then the careworn man bent down and held out his arms to receive his grandchildren for what might be the last time. Tears poured from the eyes of all three travelers.

Ethan knew their grandpa was about to leave but he still had one last question to ask. It was a matter that simply could not wait until he and his sister's hopeful, but uncertain, return to Glæm.

"Grandpa, do you regret not continuing toward Gloam when you were young?"

Emmett, with an utterly contented look on his face answered as he was turning to leave, "No son, I have no regrets." Then he disappeared into the forest, as abruptly as he had come. To Ethan and Eisley, their grandfather was a different man – he had gone from being a spunky old villager to being a spunky old adventurer. Not only had the twins' bond grown that day but now they shared a stronger tie with Emmett as well.

The weight of what lay ahead hammered down on brother and sister as they looked deep into the forest stretching before them. They were alone now – but not really alone. For much to Ethan's surprise, they did have each other.

"It's a good thing I'm getting used to surprises," said Ethan thoughtfully.

"Yeah," agreed Eisley. "At this rate, nothing will be certain tomorrow."

Chapter Four
Sleepy Turtles

The next morning the twins were roused unceremoniously by the clamorous chirping of a bird who had perched on the top of their tent.

Their rude awakening especially agitated Ethan because it interrupted a peculiar dream he'd been having. In his dream, Ethan stood in the dark surrounded by watchful eyes. The figures encircling him hadn't seemed dangerous or even scared, yet they maintained a safe distance from him. He remembered looking around for Eisley and the lantern and not being able to find either one. He had been completely alone but for the whites of the watchful eyes.

Albeit unwillingly, Ethan was conscious now and he stood to take in his surroundings, breathing the fresh morning air while looking for signs of the sun in an attempt to gauge the time. Apparently, he and Eisley woke not long after daybreak. The sun still hid below the tree line in the east.

"Trees," muttered Ethan.

All he had seen for nearly two days were trees and he longed to reach the mountains and break free from the canopy that stretched endlessly ahead. The night before, the twins saw what they thought were the first outlying mountains of the Camel Back Mountain range not far from where they camped. But from his present vantage point, Ethan could see nothing but branches. He thought it would have been better to follow his original inclination of traveling through dusk of the previous day. However, hunger and exhaustion brought them to a halt earlier than either he or his sister would have liked. In their hurry to leave the clearing with their grandfather the morning before, they had forgone any sort of meal. Emmett left the twins soon after midday, and they had decided to keep moving rather than stopping to rest. By the time early evening arrived they were famished and made the decision to set up camp.

Eisley crawled from the tent, already packed and ready for the day. She glanced at the top of the tent where the bird still sat, singing away, as if she and her brother were not even there. She marveled at the wildlife that existed in the wood. Every creature seemed to have a song here. Turning away from the happy little bird, Eisley noticed her brother peering upward. "Can you see the mountains?" She asked.

"No, not from here. I'm sure we saw them yesterday though." Ethan's stomach growled loudly. "What's for breakfast?"

"Well, we have berries or we have dried meat – your choice!" Eisley answered with mock enthusiasm.

Already, they missed their mother's cooking – one of many things they'd taken for granted.

"I guess I'll have berries. And a side of pancakes to go with them, please." Ethan half wished his sister could produce the latter from thin air. "Let's eat quickly so we can get a move on. I'm sure our family has been looking for us all night. We probably shouldn't have stayed here so long."

"As mischievous as Grandpa is becoming, he might have led them in a different direction from us," smiled Eisley. They both laughed at this notion, though neither liked the idea of their grandpa misleading their frantic parents, nor did they actually believe he would.

The twins ate in silence, listening and studying the sounds around them. And then, after packing up the camp for the second morning of their adventure, they were off.

Ethan knew the landscape that lay ahead of them in the coming days. At home, maps hung on his bedroom walls depicting Glæm and the Luminae Forest. He knew they faced at least two days' journeying, before they would reach the first of the mountains. The Camel Back Mountains were giant treeless hills that sprang up out of the forest. As a child, Ethan thought the mountains looked more like colossal turtles that had fallen asleep, and after many years turned into actual mountains. But for some reason, maybe because camels were indigenous to northern Glæm, the mountains had been named for them. When they reached the first of the humps, Ethan thought his childhood imaginings still offered a more accurate portrayal.

The siblings' calculation had not been far off. They reached the mountain they'd seen the previous day long before noon. The foot of the first mountain stood only yards away from them, jetting out steeply from the flat ground. It was as if you could pin point this exact place where the flat ground ended and the rising land began. As they surveyed this odd sight, Eisley said, "I think we should climb to the top to get a better idea of where to go next."

"My thoughts exactly," said Ethan.

They made their way toward the mountain and began to climb. It didn't take long to push through the treetops. Once above the branches, Eisley had no trouble scaling the slope of the green monstrosity. Ethan felt much more comfortable comparing his athletic prowess to Eisley's on the ground, for here, on the side of this mountain, there was no competition. Eisley sped up the hill, easily reaching the top in no time at all. When Ethan made it to the summit far behind his sister, he found her lying back in the soft grass humming a tune. He sat down beside her to catch his breath knowing the expression she wore to be a subtle form of mockery, but he said nothing of it. They sat for a while surveying the mountain range which spanned out across the southeastern skyline. Now they could see that they sat on a smaller hillock because in the distance stood mountains three times as tall, some even reaching far into the clouds. It was a strange sight to behold because not even one tree stood upon any of the hills, yet the forest grew thick on the flatlands encircling them. Ethan looked back to the north, the way they had come and near the horizon he could see the edge of Luminae Forest and what he thought to be Luminae's Town Hall, no more than a speck at the edge of the world. He was just spotting the smoke from distant chimneys all over Luminae Township when Eisley spoke his thoughts, "Look, smoke!"

Ethan looked at his sister, expecting her to be facing Luminae, as he was, but she was still turned toward the mountains. He followed her southward gaze and there he saw, high on the top of a mountain, smoke rising and curling towards the heavens. It looked very similar to the smoke coming from Luminae.

"It must be a village or something," he said excitedly.

"Do you think it's Farthenly?" asked Eisley.

"It can't be. Grandpa said that Grandma's village was to the north and east of Luminae. Maybe it's another village like Farthenly," replied Ethan.

"Hmm, I wonder how many villages there are in the mountains?" said Eisley.

"I don't know, but I think we should head in that direction," answered Ethan as he pulled out their grandfather's map. He studied the homemade sketch, periodically glancing up to survey the landscape. After a short time, Ethan pointed towards their discovery and said, "I don't think Grandpa ever traveled that far south. I'm sure he was expecting us to take the northerly path that he'd marked out for us on his map." He thought for a moment. "But, if we go towards the smoke I don't think our family will look for us there."

"That will make our chances of getting to Gloam better, don't you think?" asked Eisley.

"Yeah, I think it does."

"How far away do you think that smoke is Ethan?"

He looked back towards Luminae and compared the distance between the smoke there and the smoke on the mountain before them. "I'd say about a day's travel from here."

Eisley turned to look back towards Luminae. "We've come a long way considering how thick the forest has become."

"Yeah," agreed Ethan, getting to his feet. "And we'd better get going if we want to cover any distance today." Eisley stood as well and together they began to carefully make their way down the other side of the hillock.

The twins traveled on until the sun reached the western treetops and were soon struggling to see well enough to continue on without the lantern. Eisley turned it on by twisting the old brass knob on the top. Despite the age of the lantern the knob was in excellent working condition, clicking on with ease. The twins found it interesting that their lantern needed no external fire to be ignited. All other lanterns needed such a thing to light them. Guided by the light of the lantern, the two continued forward well into the late evening. Once they found a suitable camping spot, Ethan and Eisley stopped for the night. They left the lantern lit until they had built a small fire and pitched their tent. They hadn't noticed until turning it off that the song of animals and insects alike surrounded and pulsed around them like a hymn of nature, though now the song had all but vanished.

"That was strange," said Eisley, listening to the sudden silence.

"Yeah...very," said Ethan. "Let's try something."

Ethan grabbed the lantern and ignited the brilliant flame within. As he did, the voices of the forest creatures tore through the night like before.

"How odd," said Ethan, baffled, "I wonder why the lantern makes the animals sing?"

"Maybe it really is magical," answered Eisley. "Whatever it is though, I won't get *any* sleep with all this racket. Let's try it again tomorrow night."

Ethan extinguished the lamplight and the forest went silent. "I wonder why we didn't notice anything before?"

"I think I was too busy thinking about Grandpa's story last night to notice the animals' singing," replied Eisley.

"Yeah me too, I guess," said Ethan thoughtfully. "Let's eat and then get some rest. We have a good bit more walking to do tomorrow before we reach the village."

The twins made the best of their rations, eating the dried meat and nuts sparingly. Ethan noted the growing darkness as they lay in their tent that night. He had never been able to see this little in all his life. Only when he'd closed his eyes tight and placed them under his pillow had the darkness appeared as it did now. Yet as he readied himself for sleep he held his eyes wide open and could barely see his sister lying next to him. "So much for glowing Glæmians," he thought to himself.

Eisley was thinking about the darkness as well. "It is so much darker here than at home."

"I know. It is odd to say, but the forest has both light and darkness at the same time," answered Ethan.

"I wonder if Gloam really has no light?" asked Eisley.

42

"If the legends are true, then I'm sure there will be no light," replied her brother.

"I'm glad we have our lantern," yawned Eisley.

"Me too," yawned Ethan in response, and without much persuasion they both drifted off into a dreamless sleep.

The sun arose the next morn, and with it a rising soreness in Ethan's muscles. He had been fine so far with the walking, but yesterday's climb left him achy and stiff. Eisley, on the other hand, who was used to such exercise, woke with a lithe energy and excitement for the day's journey.

They wasted no time breaking down the camp. Ethan decided it would be better to eat on the way and so they set off, food in hand. They set a pace they hoped would bring them to the rising smoke by sundown.

Their day was spent very much like those that had preceded it: continual walking, ducking under and stepping over limbs, and occasionally cutting through vines with their small camping knife. Ethan couldn't believe he'd plunged into the depths of an unfamiliar forest with nothing more than a knife. He could have kicked himself. Though neither hoped for it, Ethan knew they needed something larger for defending themselves if the occasion ever called for it. There were really no reasons for defending oneself in Glæm because its inhabitants lived peaceably with one another; however, weapon lore was still studied by a handful of people in the land. Grandpa Charston, had been one of the few. Ethan and Eisley spent their summers at Charston and Noemi's home in a small settlement a few days' journey northeast of Luminae called Ilona. Since the time Ethan had been old enough, he'd helped his grandfather in his smithy, learning to make horseshoes, pots and pans and other things of a practical nature. What interested Charston the most, though, was sword forgery, and by extension Ethan grew familiar with the practice himself. Swords, when seldom created by his grandfather, had been requested by customers who shared the same love for such novelties as he did. Ethan had loved watching his grandfather work, and he absorbed as many details regarding the process as he could during his childhood.

Charston was one of four different smiths involved in the art of sword making as it was in Glæm. First, the Ironmaster made the steel. Second, the cutler (who was Charston) would forge, ground and heat the treated blade and then pass it along to the third smith involved, the Bladesmith. He sharpened the blade using a grinder and then fortified its strength with a series of heat treatments. Lastly, the Hiltsmith made the furniture and grip for the blade. The rare smiths who participated in this craft were spread far and wide throughout the land of Glæm. Thus, to have a sword finished properly took a lot of time as the weapon had to travel great distances to be completed. Charston had surprised Ethan one summer by making him a sword of his own, which he had never actually used. Even now the sword hung uselessly on his bedroom wall. How he longed for that weapon here in the thick of the darkening forest, even though he wouldn't know what to do with it never having trained to wield one. The twins' only weapon training had been in archery, a skill they occasionally used for hunting. It was Grandpa Emmett who typically did all the hunting for the Lambent family though.

Hours passed as Ethan and Eisley trudged through the thickening bramble, and at the close of the day, thankfully, their persistence paid off. Just as the sun began to nod off to sleep the two found themselves looking up through the trees toward what appeared to be a small settlement. They were still far enough away that they decided to wait until the next morning to travel up to the village, high above. The twins found a decent spot for setting up the tent and proceeded to make camp.

Ethan thought it would be better not to light a fire and keep their arrival quiet as long as possible. They hoped the villagers would accept them peacefully, but they didn't want to take any chances. Thankfully, winter hadn't yet arrived in Glæm, mild though it always was, and so there was no need for a fire that night anyway. They decided, instead, to take the lantern inside the tent and eat by its light before going to sleep, which seemed like a good idea at the time. What they had not anticipated was the lamplight causing the tent to radiate brightly, like a lighthouse over a dark sea at night. The lantern's beams swirled around the inside of the tent in a formless manner, heedless of the twins' frantic desire to remain hidden. Ethan quickly took hold of the strobe's source and extinguished it. Discomfited and tense, the twins ate in the darkness, hoping that the village didn't have watchman and, if they did, that those watchman hadn't seen the spectacle of light emanating from the tent in the forest below.

But they had.

Chapter Five
Balancing Act

Soon after Ethan and Eisley settled down to sleep, they were met by the sound of a gruff voice breaking into the quiet of the night. "Hey, you in there! Come out!

Frozen with terror the twins didn't move hoping that the angry voice would go away.

"There's no use stalling, you're surrounded!" came the voice again.

The twins, frightened but determined not to appear alarmed, crawled slowly out of the tent and to their feet and found themselves surrounded by a company of scruffy looking soldiers. Each one wore a primitive sort of armor consisting of thin, straight sticks strung together, which hung loosely across their chests and backs. Most had also fashioned helmets from the same type of wood, but used smaller sticks tied together to make a rather silly looking headpiece. The men gripped long spears, and although Ethan didn't think much of their armor, the sharp, shining points at the end of their spears sent a chill down his spine.

Ethan's eyes found the man shouting orders, and he was surprised to see a soldier garbed in a proper set of armor. The tall figure wore a torso piece made of metal segments overlaying one another that covered his shoulders, chest and stomach. Leather bracers and greaves covered his arms and legs, and upon his head sat a helmet that covered the whole of his face. He appeared dreadful and Ethan was certain that this man had been the one to wake them with his shouts.

The frightening figure approached the siblings, short sword in hand and demanded, "Why do you trespass in our dominion?"

Ethan instinctively slid between Eisley and the commander before answering in a stutter, "We…we didn't realize we were trespassing on someone's land."

"You are in the realm of Maridia and all travelers must be granted permission to pass through our lands," continued the leader.

"We apologi…" began Ethan.

"We saw a strange light in your camp. What was it?"

"That…was…our lantern sir," answered Ethan, struggling to speak.

"Lantern?" said the one in command, as if he didn't believe the named objected capable of such a light display. "Is it in your tent?"

Ethan and Eisley both nodded.

"Bring it to me then."

Ethan sent his sister into the tent to retrieve the lantern, and as she emerged the armored man beckoned for her to bring it to him. Ethan took the lantern from Eisley and handed it to the man, who examined the lantern thoroughly. After several moments, he turned the knob, igniting the light within. The forest lit up with a thousand rays of light that surged and swirled across the faces of the frightened company. A frenzy broke out among the soldiers as they ran about, ducking and swiping at the light with their weapons. Their leader, the one holding the lantern was the only one who remained calm. He sounded disgusted by the cowardice of his troop as he shouted, "Stop acting like a bunch of jack rabbits!" His abrupt shouting caused Ethan and Eisley to cower near the entrance of their tent. The man looked back at them then turned the lantern off and asked, "What sort of evil bewitches this lantern? Is there a spell on it?"

Ethan stood, swallowed, and through a sheer act of his will recovered his composure to answer the dreadful man. "It is not evil and there are no spells on it."

The hidden face seemed to contemplate Ethan's response, for his eyes narrowed within the helmet. He called out to his company. "Bind them and gather their belongings." Then, to the twins, "You'll be coming with us to Maridia. The Overseer will want to question you personally as to the nature of this lantern and of your intrusion in our realm."

"Please let us go!" cried Eisley, "We didn't know we were on your land. We came here because we saw the smoke on the mountaintop. We are from the town of Luminae just a few days journey from here. We meant no harm…"

"Quiet!" commanded the soldier, "Whether you meant harm are not is for the Overseer to decide."

Eisley cowered at the man's thunderous voice. Then silently she started to cry.

Ethan tried to console her, feeling much less brave than he wanted his sister to believe him to be. "Everything will be alright, Eisley. They'll take us to this *Overseer* and we'll convince him that we meant no harm." They held on to one another as two soldiers bound them in shackles and led them off into the forest.

Not far from their camp, the twins' captors met up with yet another soldier mounted atop a wagon drawn by two horses. Ethan and Eisley huddled together in the back of the wagon, fettered to its side. A narrow road ahead of them wound along the base of the mountain, and the twins watched as a smoke cloud smoldered above the mountain's peak.

"There must be a way for the horses to climb the mountain on the other side," whispered Ethan. A few soldiers repositioned themselves at the wagon's flanks while the remainder fell into place directly behind the vehicle to keep an eye on the prisoners.

The party made its way around the bottom of the mountain and then turned east, heading away from the giant hill. Three of the soldiers who had been following behind the leader left the carriage and began to scale the hillside on foot, climbing towards the smoke.

"We're not going up the hill?" whispered Eisley.

"No, I think we're going someplace else," replied Ethan just as quietly. He was careful to make sure the commander didn't overhear anything he was saying.

"I knew someone had to see the light from the lantern," continued Ethan, wishing he'd never turned the lantern on earlier that evening.

The wagon bounced across rocky terrain, moving further away from the mountain where the three men still climbed its side. The twins flailed and thudded into the wagon's side, acquiring several bruises while trying their best to keep their balance. The only way to maintain any sort of stability was by holding on to the rings protruding from the wagon's sides where their shackles hung. Ethan and Eisley's wrists, raw and bleeding, chafed painfully against their bindings. Eisley thought the commander cruel for allowing them to endure such harsh treatment. She thought of asking him to release them but remained silent, fearing his deep voice more than her injuries.

Soon the wagon met flat land, much to the relief of the twins. The trees above parted, revealing a moonless sky. This far into the Camel Back Mountains the clouds nearly enveloped the sky, but for a few sporadic holes that revealed the starry heavens above them. The clouds made the land darker than the twins had ever seen it. After having spent the day walking through the forest and the last hour wrestling to keep up their balancing act in the back of the wagon, the smooth surface that they now traveled on lulled both Ethan and Eisley into a deep sleep.

Ethan woke the next day to the sound of the two horses' hooves pounding the ground. Before even opening his eyes, his first thought was to wonder how could the soldiers possibly keep up with this pace on foot; but as the world came into focus around him, he found that the company now rode in the wagon with him and his sister. The commander sat near the front of the wagon with his helmet in his lap. The gruff man didn't look as scary as he had the night before. He had a short bushy beard that was as red as the cropped hair on the top of his head. His eyes seemed almost kind in light of day. In fact, Ethan thought the man reminded him of his own father in a strange sort of unkempt way. The commander faced the direction they were traveling, which Ethan could only guess was east, the same way they'd been traveling the night before. He turned to his sister who still slept.

He hated that she'd wake up to find herself trapped in this horrid reality – a reality brought on by his foolish desire for adventure. Ethan disliked himself in that moment, knowing that had he stayed in Glæm, his sister wouldn't be shackled and bruised across from him now. In her dreams Ethan knew Eisley would be free from this living nightmare. He would let her sleep for as long as she could.

Ethan peered toward the cloudy sky. The forest was still parted by the wide, straight road stretching out before the wagon. In the distance rose the small outline of a mountain that Ethan recognized as the place their troubles began. Apparently, they had traveled speedily through the night because they had covered a great distance. To the right and left of the wagon stood mountains at a much closer proximity. Ethan looked out past the wagon's driver as they approached the largest mountain he'd seen thus far. The wagon progressed through a valley on a road cut out by the people of Maridia, no doubt, as the commander had called the realm.

Near the top of the mountain, just below the cloud line, Ethan could make out a town. Because they were closer to their impending doom than he'd realized, he decided to wake his sister. She started to life.

"Where…where are we?" Eisley asked in a sleepy voice as she sat up and shook the grogginess away.

"I think we are near their town," Ethan answered in low voice.

The company made its way to the foot of the mountain and the wagon came to a stop. Before them stood an elaborate horse stable, which housed a dozen or so steeds. The stable looked much more like a human house in comparison to the simple stables of Luminae – it was made of large wooden planks that fit snugly together giving the horses a safe haven from the elements. It was clear from the design that the Maridians treated their animals with kindness. The Maridians' care for their prisoners seemed another matter entirely in light of the shackles the twins found themselves in at present.

As Ethan and Eisley continued to survey the area, it was the enormous contraption to the right of the stable that seized their attention. There, extending the entire height of the mountainside, ran two wooden tracks. At the bottom of the left track was a large wooden platform. The men attending the platform motioned for the carriage to move forward. The attendees led the wagon onto the raised surface, where the wagon wheels fell into small slits made especially for that purpose. The wagon carrying the twins and the soldiers boarded the mammoth lift. With a shudder the platform began to make its way up the mountain's side.

About midway up the mountain the twins noticed a platform mirroring their own, headed down a track to their right. It was loaded with large stone cubes that stood about a foot in height – a counterweight. Ethan was amazed at the ingenuity of the mechanism.

In minutes, the company reached the top and they continued their journey up a narrow road alongside the top of the mountain that rose into the clouds to their left. The party turned one last bend in the road where it widened as the town came into view.

Maridia was much larger than the twins expected. In their minds, they were headed towards something like they'd imagined Farthenly to be – in a few words, small and rural. The town was well fortified. An outer wall of two story buildings surrounded the town, and Ethan noticed windows only on their second floors in order to keep the town better protected from trespassers. Ethan thought this town was much larger than Luminae. As they reached the city gate, two guards, wearing the same wooden armor as their captors walked towards them. The commander of their party donned his helmet and, jumping off the wagon, went to speak privately with the city guards. One of the two watchmen ran off into the town while the other waved them through.

As the wagon passed under the open archway, Ethan could tell he'd been deceived by the outer wall as to the size of this town. Maridia was much smaller on the inside. Ethan had expected street upon street to line their way towards the middle of the town, though as they entered, he could see the entire inhabitance directly before them. Maridia was no more than a large outer circle of tall homes and businesses overlooking a fountain, which stood waterless in the middle of the enclosure. On the far side of the wall, directly across from the gate stood the tallest part of the structure, where a man dressed all in black stood. As the twins drew closer to him they noticed he looked a bit comical, having fluffy, snow-white hair that stood up in all directions with thick sideburns to match. The man appeared old, but in good health only for a funny little belly that protruded from his otherwise wiry frame. All in all, this foe seemed a much less formidable one than the red-bearded man on the wagon.

The wagon came to a stop directly in front of him. "Hello," he said, addressing the twins. "My name is Alaric Jukes. I am the Overseer of Maridia." The Overseer gazed upon Ethan and Eisley and then turned towards the commander of the little rabble. "Deerborn, these are but children. Did you think it absolutely necessary to shackle them? They do not appear to be murderous villains, to me."

Deerborn, as was his given name, was taken aback by the sudden attack on his judgment. He opened his mouth to speak but was interrupted by the Overseer who spoke to the twins again.

"Under normal circumstances I'd be extending a warm welcome to visitors of our secluded city. However, I believe my courtesies might fall on deaf ears, given your present state and the utter lack of care on our part." At this statement Jukes shot an exasperated look at Deerborn. "Guards, free these children and allow them to be cleaned up." The surprised soldiers hurried to do the man's bidding. He continued. "You are twins, are you not?"

"Yes, sir," they answered together. Hope rose in the hearts of Ethan and Eisley as the threat of death and doom lifted. Behind them a sizable crowd of onlookers had begun to form.

"What are your names?" asked the Overseer.

"Ethan and Eisley Lambent," they said in turn.

Jukes' eyes widened as if he'd only now begun to really listen. "I'm sorry, can you repeat your surname once again?"

"Lambent," they said in unison.

Jukes grew quiet, lost in thought. "Hmm, well...yes, we will have things to discuss then – that is once you have been properly seen to."

Deerborn held up the lantern. "They were carrying this," he said in an agitated tone, igniting the lantern himself. Even in the daylight the rays of light were brilliant, shimmering and bouncing off of the walls of citadel that encircled them. The curious bystanders began to scatter and a few women shrieked at the spectacle. One by one the mass returned to their previous business most likely wishing they hadn't been so nosy.

Jukes stood looking stupefied and muttered, "The lantern is real?"

Chapter Six
A Deadly Poison

It took a moment for Jukes to regain his composure. Clearing his voice he said, "Um…yes, well…much to talk about indeed. Go on, Deerborn, get these two cleaned up and bring them back to me. They will dine with me this evening."

It was clear that Deerborn regretted his decision to bind the twins. Once Jukes retreated into the tallest of the buildings, Deerborn faced the twins. Eyes softening, the man said, "I'm sorry for chaining you to the wagon young ones. It was hard to judge your age in the poor light of evening and with the lantern…well…doing its…magic, I overreacted. Then, when I got a good look at the two of you this morning I thought to release you from your bondage but we were close to Maridia and I feared for your safety. I thought you might try to escape while we were on the lift. More than one unfortunate soul has fallen to their death from that machine and I didn't want you to go hurting yourselves."

Ethan could see the kindness in Deerborn's eyes, just as he had on their journey to Maridia that morning.

Eisley had always been a good judge of character, and she felt that Deerborn really was sorry for their treatment. She rushed to his side and wrapped an arm around him. The man nearly stood twice her height. "It's alright, Deerborn. We forgive you."

Deerborn's face turn as red as his beard at this gesture. "Dear child, how could my judgment have been so bad?"

The man still seemed to scold himself over his choice, and something in Ethan desired to put him at ease. "It really is alright Deerborn. Everyone make mistakes." He swallowed. "I think I might have made a big one in leaving home in the first place."

Deerborn handed the lantern to Eisley as he moved toward the front of the cart and began to loosen the bridle on the horse nearest to him. "You said you are from Glæm, correct?"

"Yes, we live in Luminae," answered Ethan.

"We will do everything in our power to get you home safely young Lambents," said Deerborn nodding. The man took Ethan's hand to shake it in a sign of friendship. Deerborn noticed the cuts that the shackles had made on both Ethan and Eisley's wrists and grimaced. "I'm sorry for the injuries you received in my care. I will make sure the town's healer sees to your wounds before I bring you back to the Overseer."

Eisley smiled her thanks.

Deerborn had completely changed in a matter of minutes. One moment he'd seemed like a giant grizzly bear ready to attack at their every word and now he seemed like a bear cub trapped in a grizzly's body.

Just then a servant arrived and led the siblings into the side entrance of the Overseer's home. There the twins bathed and dressed in new garments, given as a gift from their host. The cloth, stitched by Maridia's tailor, was soft but the colors harsh. The tunics were grey and the pants, black. Very unlike their old clothes consisting of warm, earthen colors. Refreshed and enlivened, they were escorted by Deerborn to the healer.

The healer was a trim and proper old man who spoke with the eloquence of one in his profession, having excellent bed-side manners. The healer appeared to be training an apprentice in the art of mending wounds with herbs and elixirs. The younger man watched with careful eyes as the elder tended to the twins' wounds. Ethan wondered if magic of any sort was used in his practice. He'd read of healers in ages past who'd done things of that nature. But it appeared that this physician used only remedies found in the Light-given soil to nurse his patients back to health. On Ethan and Eisley's wounds he used a green paste that was cool to the touch and stung when first applied. Then he bandaged the wounds with large leaves, folding them over thrice upon themselves, and wrapping them around the infected wrists. Once their treatment was complete, the twins bid the healer and his apprentice farewell with many thanks and followed Deerborn back to the tall building opposite the town gate. The Overseer awaited their arrival, just inside the door. Ethan wondered if he had been watching for their return.

"Ah, Children," said Jukes, "I hope you have been treated well *since arriving here.*" He directed a harsh glance towards Deerborn. Ethan and Eisley both felt sorry that Deerborn was still being reprimanded by the Overseer.

"Really, sir," began Eisley. "We understand, now, why Deerborn chained us up. We've forgiven him."

The Overseer appeared skeptical of Eisley's comment, forcing a smile. "Well then, let me formally welcome you to Maridia. You are free to stay and linger in our hilltop haven for as long as you like, leaving some of the happiness that you bring. We have many things to discuss, but first, we will dine."

The siblings were ushered to a room with a long table, big enough to seat eight. The dinner was informal. The aristocracy of this town had simple cutlery, using hand-crafted wooden forks and spoons. The party drank from short wooden cups that the servants kept filled to the brim with piping hot tea. Jukes sat opposite Ethan and Eisley as they all dined on roasted pheasant, potatoes and a bitter leafy green vegetable that was foreign to the twins. Ethan and Eisley were famished and ate three helpings each, grateful for their first proper meal in nearly a week. After they had supped, the company retreated to the Overseer's study.

The room was much like one would imagine a town-leader's study to be. Dark wood covered the floor, walls and ceiling, and dim, flickering lamps barely gave off enough light to illuminate the room. As the twins stood in the doorway, awaiting directions, Jukes took the seat behind a large desk with the same deep reddish-brown colors as the rest of the room. The desk sat to the left of the entryway, facing tall windows that overlooked the waterless fountain in the middle of town. The study was on the fourth floor of the building, which probably wasn't practical for meeting with guests, but it had the best view and vantage point of any place in town. In fact, as Ethan neared the window for a better look, he could see clear over the gate and its surrounding buildings all the way down to the bend in the road where the twins had first seen the citadel up close. Ethan thought that the Overseer had probably stood here to watch for their arrival. Eisley joined her brother and together they marveled at the scenery beyond the fortress walls. They could see the valley they passed through earlier that day. Smoke rose near the western horizon atop the mountain where they'd been taken prisoner the night before. The sun sank slowly behind the smoky mountain, casting brilliant pink and purple hues across the thickening clouds.

"The mountains look so beautiful from here," commented Eisley, mesmerized.

"Yes, it is quite a sight," said Jukes. "As is the view from over here." He motioned behind him toward matching windows behind the desk where he sat. "Come have a look," he beckoned.

The window revealed the eastern sky. From this direction, the clouds were thicker and darker than they'd been on the other window, seeming nigh impenetrable. The scenery below the clouds looked familiar. The road running through the valley extended out in a mirror image of the opposite side and also led to a mountain with smoke rising from its crest.

"Are the two mountains at the ends of the valley lookout posts?" asked Ethan.

"Yes, we have observation towers on both mountains," answered the old man with an amused look on his face. "You are very astute for your age aren't you?" Ethan shrugged, a little embarrassed.

Then Jukes pointed to a map of the area on his study wall. The cartogram depicted a drawing of the mountain where Maridia was positioned, symbolized by a circle with an "M" inside it. Stretching out on either side of the icon were two long straight lines, running parallel to one another – the road. A circled "W" to the west and a circled "E" to the east marked the mountains where the lookout posts stood at the far ends of the valley road. The drawing was simple but had been masterfully drafted and scaled to size. It was incredibly precise, especially in comparison to the map of Luminae that hung from Ethan's bedroom wall.

"And you created the pass between the three mountains?" asked Ethan staring back and forth between the map and the window.

"Well, no," answered Jukes. "You see, the valleys and flatlands have been like this since before our ancestors came to this mountain. We only take advantage of what nature created."

"Nature created?" questioned Eisley.

"Ah, yes. The two of you are from Glæm, so naturally you would think all things are created by the light," answered Jukes. "But, here we are not so sure that even the light wasn't just the product of a random process of nature like everything else. Including ourselves, I might add."

"That's ridiculous," said Ethan, "the Light existed before everything else. It wasn't some random process. It created everything, including us."

"I understand why you would think this, young one," said Jukes, patronizing Ethan. "However, our perspective is much different here. Our land lies between Glæm and Gloam. You see, you've grown up in a place of undying light and have known nothing else. We have seen both the light *and* the darkness from here."

This train of thought seemed utterly absurd. Ethan's face reddened, and he was visibly flustered by his beliefs being questioned.

"My dear boy, please don't get upset," said Jukes. "I believe that we can both be right. There is always more than one side to every reality. For you, having never seen the darkness in your land of eternal light, you'd have no reason to question the nature of things beyond what you think to be true. Because we see the darkness and the light, we ask the question, if the light truly created everything, then why does the darkness exist as well? Why does the darkness even exist at all?"

The Overseer seemed to pause for effect.

"Darkness is the antonym of light, my dear child, and it can be a frightening thing. Since the light and dark both coexist, doesn't it stand to reason that both were created by something else? That is, if they were created at all."

Ethan remained silent.

"We feel we are the most gifted of all people to sit between the two lands where we can see the bigger picture. Anyhow, this discussion is of no great consequence here and now. Like I said before, we are probably both right in some way. Who can say?"

For Ethan this subject was of dire consequence. The Light had been the essence of his entire life and now it was being questioned in such a nonchalant manner. This discussion was far from over. Eisley, however, was completely disinterested by the conversation, gazing out the window towards Gloam.

"Are you alright my dear girl?"

"Um...yes sir, I'm fine. I was just wondering, do those clouds stay over Gloam all the time?" answered Eisley.

"Yes...they do. Some believe they are held there by magic. Others, like myself, think otherwise. Or at least I thought so, until today." The Overseer eyed the lantern hanging from Eisley's hand. She hadn't let it out of her sight since entering Maridia.

Eager to address his real reason for inviting the twins to his study that evening, the Overseer abruptly changed the subject. "Speaking of magic, I'm most interested in how you came by this lantern." He placed a hand on the twin's heirloom. "We have heard stories of a lantern like this before and it just so happens that the character in those stories bore the same last name as the two of you."

Had the people of this hidden town actually heard of their ancestor?

"You know of The Boy of Legend?" asked Ethan.

"Well…yes," answered Jukes, "but only because of *another* Lambent."

What other Lambent could this man have heard of? Of Course. Earnest Lambent. It had to be. Had he come as far as Maridia?

"Earnest?" asked Ethan.

"So you are kin to him," asked the Overseer.

The twins nodded.

"Astounding. What are the odds? Tell me young ones, what brings you into the mountains, so far away from your home?" said Jukes, reaching out for the lantern. "Is this really the lantern of Riley Lambent?"

The twins feared telling Alaric Jukes too much. Even the people of Glæm didn't know of the lantern. Yet, he had been so gracious, giving them food and clothing, treating their wounds and even sharing his own home. After all, he was already aware of Riley, the lantern and Earnest, so there weren't many secrets left to keep. Plus, he didn't live in Glæm, so what did it really matter?

And so reluctantly, Ethan and Eisley recounted their family's history, speaking of Riley's adventures and the disappearance of Earnest. They told the old man of the Awakening and their plan to venture into the mountains and ultimately into Gloam. Jukes was familiar with the latter part of their travels, as his Captain of the Guard had been the one to force them into their present situation. The man listened intently, eyes aglow with great curiosity.

When the siblings finished their tale Ethan asked, "What do you know of Earnest Lambent?" Any word of Earnest's fate would be appreciated. Ethan hoped he'd be able to share this with his family one day.

"Earnest Lambent is a name known by most of our people. Long ago, when my forefathers governed this town, Earnest came from the west, out of Glæm, in search of the very thing you now seek. Gloam. Archibald Jukes, my great, great, great grand-father, received Earnest into our community and gave him provisions for his journey eastward, into the darkness. Archibald warned him of the danger he would face upon entering Gloam." Jukes' eyes narrowed. "Alas, my forefather's warning fell on deaf ears, for Earnest Lambent ventured off into the dark land only to return weeks later nearly dead. In fact, he passed away here in this very house."

Ethan swallowed his fear. "How did he die?"

"Poisoned, I believe it was," recalled Jukes. "Yes, poisoned by a dart of some sort."

"Who would do that?" asked Eisley, a chill in her voice.

"Oh…they have many names," said the old man, "to some they are known as nomads or guardians, mostly they are referred to as Watchers because that is what Earnest Lambent called them."

"Watchers," repeated Ethan. "What were they watching?"

"Well…Earnest Lambent in this case," said Jukes. "They were watching Earnest Lambent."

"What are they?" said Eisley, trembling.

"No one knows exactly. We only know that they roam through the darkness, guarding the lands from something. Or at least they did in Earnest Lambent's time," answered Jukes. "What's even more peculiar is that, it is believed, Gloamers do not even use the sense of sight due to the utter darkness that surrounds them. So in all actuality, the name your ancestor gave to these creatures might not even be accurate." The old man pondered this for a moment. "Anyhow, it was Earnest's death at the hands of the Watchers that drove us to build the eastern lookout. The Maridians were afraid the Watchers might try to attack, and so we erected the tower." Jukes stood now, looking out the window behind his desk towards the smoke rising on the mountain in the distance.

"Why did you build the other lookout?" asked Ethan, gesturing back towards the direction they'd come from.

"We built it because of Earnest," answered the man. "Our people's anxiety grew after Earnest's death. The tower to the west was built to watch for more of your kind," he said looking toward the twins, a smile on his face. "I'd say it is doing its job rather well. Though, ironically, you're the first Glæmians to travel into our domain since Earnest Lambent."

Jukes nodded toward the lantern. "Now, what of this lantern? Is it actually magic, as Riley's story implies?"

"I don't think the lantern is really *magical*, though we have noticed odd things happening with it," said Ethan.

Eisley looked skeptical of Ethan's comment, but the Overseer didn't notice.

"Like what?" asked Jukes, the curious glow spreading through his entire countenance.

"Well for one," Eisley said, "every time the lantern is lit, the animals in the forest around it seem to get...louder."

"Hmm...that's something, though what it would signify I can't imagine," said Jukes. "What else?"

"I'm sure you've noticed the strange way that the light shines out of it," answered Ethan, thinking back to their meeting.

"Yes, yes I have, but again I wouldn't consider that to be magic of any sort. Not by my understanding of magic, anyway. I would think it had more to do with its construction and less with enchantments. Are these the only things you've noticed?"

The twins nodded.

"That's a shame. I was hoping for more. It just goes to show you that maybe there is less to the notion of an all-powerful light than you may think."

Ethan wondered that the man could be so sure of himself. But wasn't *he* too so sure of *himself*. How could two different views both be right when they completely contradict one another? This new philosophy deserved some more thought.

Jukes stood and gazed into the twilight. "It's getting late and I'm sure you two would like a proper night's sleep, in a bed, after so many nights of sleeping sacks and hard ground. Come with me."

He led the twins down the hallway to the staircase, and down to the second floor where a spare bedroom had been prepared for them. The room was cozy, with long thick curtains closed over the windows, identical to those of the study two floors above. Two beds flanked a large fireplace that stood in the middle of the wall opposite the door. A roaring fire blazed in its belly.

"I trust you will find this room more than suitable for your stay with us," said Jukes.

"Yes sir, we will," answered Eisley, ready to retire for the night.

"We are thankful for your hospitality," added Ethan.

"Well then," smiled Jukes, "there are things I'd like to show you still. But that can wait for tomorrow. Good night then."

"Good night," echoed the twins.

The Overseer closed the door behind him and the twins made their way into the room. As they neared the warm hearth, they noticed that all of their belongings had been brought here. Their sleeping sacks and clothes had been washed and neatly folded. These items lay next to their carryalls and as they inspected the bags, the contents appeared to be untouched.

Brother and sister crawled wearily into the warmth of thick covers and prepared for sleep. While they lay there, each going over the events of the day in their minds, Ethan asked, "What did you think about the things Jukes said about nature being the creator?"

"I thought it was sad," said Eisley.

"So you think he was wrong?"

"Very much so," she replied with resolve. "You don't think he's right do you?"

"No, I don't think he's right," answered Ethan. "Still, I've never had anyone question what I've been taught before. I have to consider his side."

Eisley shot up in her bed, defensive. "You can't be serious. We've lived in the light our whole life. Surely you know our parents wouldn't feed us lies!"

"They hid the truth of Riley Lambent from us didn't they?" combated Ethan, his voice rising.

"Well...yes. And with good cause, I might add, considering our present whereabouts. Besides, it wasn't like they were going to keep it from us forever. We know now, don't we?"

Ethan wished he hadn't brought the subject up. "I've already said that I don't think the Overseer is right. I just need to *consider* the idea. Just give me time to sort it out."

Eisley dropped her head back onto her pillow without saying another word. Soon she drifted off to sleep. But Ethan lay awake for hours contemplating the new ideas of Alaric Jukes and the Maridians. Ethan didn't recognize that the Overseer had injected a poison into his mind, potentially posing more danger than the deadly toxin that took the life of Earnest Lambent. For, to lose one's physical life can never compare to the loss of one's soul. There in the quiet of the night, the lethal elixir spread through him, and Ethan fell asleep doubting everything he'd ever known.

Chapter Seven
Elderly Acrobatics

The following morning came without the fear of the previous one. Instead of hunger and soreness and bouncing in the back of a wagon, the twins woke to the smell of breakfast cooking in Jukes' home. They dressed quickly and made their way to the dining room. Ethan was delighted to find the table stacked high with plates of blueberry pancakes, bacon and eggs. Jukes and a newcomer joined the twins for breakfast. It was a girl who looked to be a few years older than the twins. She had long dark brown hair, like them, but her complexion was fairer. Ethan found himself staring at the girl as she made her way to the table. Eisley noticed Ethan's gaze and saw that the girl was looking at him in a similar manner. Embarrassed by her brother's ogling, Eisley kicked his shin beneath the table. Ethan bounced off his chair, hitting the underside of the table with his knees. Pancakes flew this way and that. His face turned bright red, as did Eisley's. She hadn't meant to cause such a scene.

"Are you quite okay my dear boy?" asked Jukes.

Ethan responded under his breath, "I'm fine." At the same time he threw a sharp look in Eisley's direction. She mouthed an apology back at him.

"Good, Good. Let me introduce my daughter – this is Delia." He placed his hand on his daughter's shoulder.

"Good day to you," Delia answered shyly with a slight curtsy.

Jukes continued, "When I learned your age last night I thought to introduce you to my Delia. She is just a year older than yourselves."

Ethan was blushing too much to respond.

"I have some meetings to attend this morning, so I've asked Delia to accompany you today. I told you last night there were some things I wanted to show you. One of these items is in the town library, and the other is outside the walls of the citadel," said the man. "Delia will take you out later, and I will escort you to the library after breakfast."

After stuffing themselves once again, the Overseer and his daughter led Ethan and Eisley across the surprising bustle of the town-circle to one of the lower two-story buildings that made up a part of the outer wall. As they crossed, the Maridians greeted Alaric and Delia but only shot inquisitive looks at the twins. Their destination had a wooden sign above the door with the word LIBRARY painted on it in faded gold lettering. The four stepped through the doorway.

The library was one large, open room reaching into the second floor of the building. All four walls were covered in books from floor to ceiling. In the middle of the aged archive was an old oak table. Ethan's eyes lit up hungrily at the wealth of knowledge spread before him.

"G'mornin', Alaric. G'mornin', Miss Delia," said a voice from the right of the entryway. The twins turned to find a little old woman barely tall enough to see over the counter she stood behind.

"Good morning, Miss Naava," answered father and daughter in unison.

"Who might these two be?" asked the little old lady, looking toward the strangers.

"This is Ethan and Eisley *Lambent*," replied Jukes.

"Lambent, did'y say?" questioned the astonished lady. She hurried around the counter to face the twins, placing her spectacles onto her nose as she came. She took a long hard look the twins, then, giving a big toothless smile, she said, "Well, I never thought the day'd come that I'd see a Lambent come through town, much less two of'em."

Eisley giggled.

"Hello, the name's Miss Naava," said the lady raising her hand in greeting.

Ethan and Eisley exchanged pleasantries and then Miss Naava turned to face Jukes. "I'm guess'n you came for the journal then, did ya?"

He nodded.

"Well," said Miss Naava. "Come on then."

The visitors followed the lady to the back of the library, where she turned right and headed towards the far corner. Tall brass ladders lined the shelves here and there, one of which Miss Naava began to climb.

The sight was amusing, to say the least. Everyone fought to hide their smiles as the lady made her way up the rungs. With each step, Miss Naava caused the wheeled ladder to roll back and forth along the track it was attached to. The scene reminded Ethan and Eisley of an act in the traveling circus they had attended long ago.

"Shouldn't one of us get the book she's looking for?" whispered Eisley, exceedingly concerned for the elderly acrobat.

"You could try but she'd push you off the ladder if you set foot on it," answered Delia, with a barely audible giggle. "She practically lives here and doesn't allow her customers to get the books for themselves. She has spent a lifetime categorizing this library and doesn't trust anyone to retrieve even one volume from the shelves."

This was the first time Delia had actually spoken more than a few words to the twins and Ethan was enraptured by the sound of her voice.

"Where did all of these books come from?" asked Ethan. "We have a library in Luminae but there are nowhere near this many books." He was genuinely curious but secretly he just wanted to her Delia speak again.

Delia blushed, being addressed directly by Ethan. "A few of the books actually came from your land. Most of them were written here, though."

"What? How is that possible? There can't have been enough people living here to create all these books. That would take..."

"Ages?" said Jukes. "It *has* taken ages. Maridia is nearly as old as Glæm, maybe even older. We have had many scholars born and bred in our modest town. We pride ourselves on the intellect of our people. Learning is a speciality of ours, in fact, next door to the library, here, is our university. I'd love to show it to you sometime, if you stay long enough."

Ethan was amazed by the news of such a school. In Glæm they were only found in the Shining City, not in smaller towns. Glæmians were properly educated, though this education took place at home, at the family level. It seemed the Maridians strived to know the world to the best of their ability – something Ethan longed for as well. Ethan found himself hoping he and Eisley might delay their journey and stay in Maridia a little longer. He started to day-dream of reading all the books around him.

As Miss Naava climbed down, Eisley asked, "Are any of these books from Gloam?"

"Gloam? Ha, 'course not. Don't y'know child? Those Gloamers live in the dark. They've got no way'ove writin'."

"How do they keep records or histories then?" asked Ethan, startled at the thought of a society without books.

"No one knows. Our people do not travel into Gloam, and so far the Gloamers have kept away from us," answered Jukes.

When Miss Naava stepped off of the last rung she tipped backward and lost her balance. Ethan and Delia caught her together and helped her to an upright position.

Ethan was suddenly aware that he was standing face to face with Delia and he withdrew awkwardly. Delia grinned.

"Thank you," said the old lady. "My balance ain't as good as it use'ta be. Anyway, here's the book you wanted."

She handed Ethan a tattered leather bound book held together by new twine.

"What is this?" asked Ethan.

"The Journal of Earnest Lambent," responded Jukes.

The world around Ethan disappeared as he reached for the chronicle. Spellbound, he made his way toward the empty table, gripping the journal tightly in his hands.

Chapter Eight
The Journal of Earnest Lambent

Ethan sat down at the table in a frenzied state as he fingered the journal's bindings, trying to open it. Eisley calmly sat down quietly next to her brother and watched as he tried to shake the twine free of the book.

"Here, let me help." Eisley seized the book from his trembling hands. Patiently, she untied the knots that held the string in place. Once she'd freed the book from its bonds, she handed it back to her brother, warning him to be careful not tear the book apart in his excitement.

Ethan opened the book cautiously, now fearing for the condition of the journal. The first page was blank, as one may often find in a book, so Ethan turned to the next and read.

The Journal of Earnest Lambent

Ethan and Eisley looked at one another in wonder. Displayed before them was their ancestor's very own handwriting. They turned the page.

The 1st day of the 3rd cycle of Vergance, our greatest moon, in the 3446th year of Glæm.

My name is Earnest Lambent. I am eleven years old. I have decided to leave home and so I am starting this journal to keep track of my adventures. My ancestor, Riley Lambent is the reason I've decided to leave. Only weeks ago Mother and Father told me that the Boy of Legend was a part of our family. The Legend says that Riley left his home in search of grand adventures at the age of thirteen. I know that I haven't yet reached this age but after finding out that this boy was a part of my own family I want to go in search of adventures just the same. I am leaving before dawn tomorrow. First, I'll journey to Luminae Township, where I plan to buy goods for the journey with the money I have earned on the farm during harvesting time. I plan to enter the forest from Luminae and follow the course marked out by Riley Lambent himself, in his own journal, given to me by my parents nearly a fortnight ago. Father told me that the journal has been passed down through the Lambent family for hundreds of years. I have spent the whole month studying his journal and plan to follow it as closely as possible. I will miss my family yet still I must go.

Earnest Lambent

"He had Riley's Journal?" whispered Ethan.

"I wonder if it is here in this library?" Eisley was equally awed at the idea.

"You can be certin' that it's not." answered the toothless Miss Naava. "I know ev'ry book on ev'ry shelf in this place."

"I don't believe Earnest ever wrote of its whereabouts either," added Jukes.

"Riley's accounts are actually lost then," declared Eisley.

The silence in the room lingered for a few seconds before the Overseer sighed.

"Well, I'm off to a day of endless meetings. The town counsel wants to know more about the two of you. I trust you will be fine in my absence."

The twins nodded in response and thanked him for his help. Jukes exited the library leaving the three youths and Miss Naava, the latter of whom set about asking the twins a series of questions about their lives before poking off toward the front counter, mumbling about Lambents and legends all the way.

Ethan turned to Delia and said, "I know you have something else to show us but would you mind if we stayed here for a while and read over the journal?"

"That's alright with me. I have some things to do around the house anyway so I'll come back in a while to check on you," answered Delia. "Oh, and I'll tell Miss Naava you'll be staying on my way out."

"Thanks," said Ethan, ogling again.

Ethan looked at his sister who smiled smugly.

"What?" cried Ethan.

"Boys. *That's* what!" said Eisley.

Embarrassed but trying to shrug it off he turned his attention back to the journal. Eisley redirected her own thoughts and inched closer to her brother to get a better view as well.

Scanning over the next few entries, the twins found that Earnest had traveled, almost exactly, the same route they had taken to get to the valley leading to Maridia. They then discovered that Maridia stood in very much the same condition in Earnest's time as it did now. Earnest wrote of Riley's reference to the mountain town, dating it back further still. Though, apparently, Riley had skirted the town out of some unnamed fear, whereas Earnest had not.

There was a brief entry concerning the townspeople and as Ethan turned the page he found a gap in the dates. Where the previous page had given a date a few weeks following the very first entry, the next page was written nearly three years later.

"Huh. I guess he decided to stay here for a while," said Eisley, following along with her brother.

"Maybe he was drawn to this library," Ethan replied, looking around, still in awe of the collection of knowledge.

"Kind of like you are."

"Yeah," agreed Ethan. "Like I am. Are you going to attack me again, like you did last night?"

"Attack? I did nothing of the sort," she retorted. "I was only shocked that a man you'd just met could possibly make you question everything you've ever believed. I meant nothing by the library bit, you're just oversensitive for some reason."

"Oversensitive? What are you going on about? You know as well as I do that I question everything I study!" Ethan's voice grew louder.

"Yes I know brother, but you've never once questioned the power that holds it all together," answered Eisley in a low voice, trying to guide Ethan volume.

"No one's ever given me a reason to, until now," he said, voice still rising. "You know maybe if you used your brai..."

Miss Naava interrupted their argument with a resounding shush that brought the twins' argument to a screeching halt.

Red-faced and annoyed, Ethan whispered, "Can we please just read the journal? We are uncovering a piece of our family's history here and I'd like to continue."

Eisley said nothing but nodded her head, teary eyed.

Ethan knew he had gone too far. He hadn't yelled at his sister since they were young. He turned to her with a silent apology and she nodded again, tears now on her cheeks.

Eisley knew what he was going to say before Miss Naava interrupted. "If you used your brain instead of your heart." Ethan kidded with this saying in the past, but only lovingly. She knew she had a tendency of following her heart over her head, yet it had never caused her problems. Eisley couldn't believe Ethan would go so far as to say something like that after dragging her halfway to Gloam. But she knew he hadn't actually dragged her anywhere. She'd followed him wholeheartedly. It was her own fault that she was here. She noticed that Ethan had stopped on one particular page of the journal, and curiosity led her back to the travels of Earnest Lambent...

The 18th day of the 7th cycle of Vergance, our greatest moon, in the 3451st year of Glæm.

I have left the town were I've stayed for four years and have decided to venture into Gloam. I have already traveled as far west as the edge of the forest, having left the last of the mountains yesterday evening. It is darker here than I have ever known the world could possibly be. The clouds are a dark red color like that of blood. No sunlight penetrates their cover; no light brightens the land I now stand and attempt to look out across. The trees have all died here on the edge of the forest due to the lack of sunlight, I would wager. By the light of my lantern it appears that the ground is nearly dried up. As I close this entry, I truly question my desire to enter herein. No good can come of this.

Earnest Lambent

The 20th day of the 7th cycle of Vergance, our greatest moon, in the 3451st year of Glæm.

I have been in Gloam for two days now. The first day was quite uneventful - I saw nothing by the light of my lamp and heard nothing. Though this morning when I arose, there was a strange flakey substance lying everywhere on the ground. I dared not touch it anymore than I had to in order to retrieve my sleeping sack from the ground. By what I guessed to be midday (I have no reference) the peculiar matter had completely dissolved away. I will investigate more tomorrow. I sit now in the light of my lantern and take note of a strange scuttling sound just beyond the reach of the light. It sounds as if it is human; though, I have called to it and there has been no response.

Earnest Lambent

The 21st day of the 7th cycle of Vergance, our greatest moon, in the 3451st year of Glæm.

Today, if it can truly be called day, was filled with many interesting occurrences. First, I decided to inspect the flaky material on the ground as it had returned. Apparently the ground produces this substance within the time of the sun's cycle, for when I awoke this morn it was all around me again. I held a piece and it was more solid than I'd originally surmised, though it still broke apart easily. Second, the noise in the darkness never left while I lay in my sleeping sack. It made it very difficult to fall asleep; however, at some point I did. When I awoke this morning the sound was not to be heard. Later in the day the noise returned - around the time I was eating my midday meal. It sounded like it was moving at an impossibly fast pace all around me. Oddly enough it never entered the light. Only minutes ago the creature called out to me. It asked me who I was and what my business was in Gloam. I'm ashamed to say that I was frightened at first, having heard no one's voice beside my own for weeks on end. I told it that I was merely a traveler seeking out the source of the darkness. It asked me my name and I gave it. Then I asked the same in return. It replied, "Llebmac." Then it said no more but ran off into the distance.

A few notes on the mysterious Llebmac:

I. *It sounded nearly human, though more eloquent, almost singing rather than talking.*

II. *It did not inquire of the light from my lantern, which is much different from Riley's own account. Perhaps Riley's journey to this light forsaken land is still remembered by the inhabitants here. How? I cannot say, for in all my studies over the past four years, concerning what little is known of the Gloamers, there is no evidence that these dark dwellers keep records or writings. This is understandable due to the oppressive darkness that seems to swallow all happiness.*

III. Even after a peaceful (be it ever so odd) introduction, the Gloamer still never revealed itself to me.

Tomorrow, I will attempt more dialogue with this Llebmac.

-Earnest Lambent

It is the 22nd day, I believe, though I'm not sure how long I slept. I was awakened in the night by the creature Llebmac. He didn't step into the light but he did manage to hit me in the temple with a small pebble. The Gloamer sounded agitated at this meeting. He bade me leave quickly for there were some who were coming to dispose of me, as he said. I thanked him for his warning and decided it best to begin my trek back towards Maridia, where I intend to study these new discoveries with those I count among my friends. I have halted now to rest as I have been moving rather quickly to make it back to the safety of the trees before these others can reach me. If they do not find me I will write again.

Earn...

I write for what may be the last time. I'm not sure of the day or time now. I sit in the forest, near the base of the mountain that rests closest to Gloam. It is still a week or more of a journey to the town and in my current condition possibly even longer. The following is brief account since my previous entry:

As I sat writing the last letter I began to hear many different noises surrounding me, they sounded similar to Llebmac yet much quicker and much more aggressive in their movement. I found that they actually were more aggressive, for within minutes of encircling me they began to edge closer to the light - close enough for me to see the whites of their eyes. Even so they wouldn't enter the light enough for me to get a good look at them, though I could tell they stood as humans do. Because they would not enter the light, I thought to use it as a makeshift form of defense, having not the wits to bring a weapon of any sort with me. I was able to use the light to my advantage for a while and took off in a westward direction, following the markers I'd left to find my way out. However, soon the attackers became privy to my tactic and chose other means of trying to dispose of me. I heard small objects rushing past my head as I ran franticly. Just as I was reaching the first signs of the Deadwood forest, I was struck in the leg by a small dart that hurt like nothing I'd ever experienced before. The Watchers, as I have decided to call them, have not appeared to follow me into the forest. Though, it is highly possible that they have already accomplished their wicked purpose, for my leg seems to be losing all feeling. There was a poison of some sort on that projectile, I am sure of it. Now I make my way towards Maridia, in hopes that I will at least live long enough to be discovered for the sake of my findings.

Earnest Lambent

Ethan turned the page to find that the entry he and Eisley had just read was, in fact, the final entry of Earnest Lambent. The twins sat in silence as the weight of what they had just discovered pressed down upon them, taking root in reality.

"I need some fresh air," said Eisley, finally.

"Yeah, me too," agreed Ethan.

As they passed Miss Naava she whispered, "I'm sorry." They were sure she had read the journal too. Most likely, all the people of Maridia had read it and now here, finally, Earnest Lambent's own kin knew the truth of his fate. And a horrible fate it was.

They stood speechless outside the library, taking in the warm afternoon sun, shrouded by clouds as it was, watching the townsfolk going about their daily tasks. Every once and a while someone would shoot a curious glance in their direction, though no one stopped to inquire about them. The twins continued to stand there, still as statues, saying very little to one another until they were eventually met by Delia. She approached them cautiously, understanding, like the old librarian, the solemn looks upon the twins' faces.

Ethan turned to her, losing all bashfulness. "Your father told us that Earnest died in your home. Did he make it back on his own or was he found by your people?"

"He made it back on his own, but barely," answered Delia, eyes toward the ground. "He died within a day of returning."

"Does the graveyard lie outside the city walls?" asked Ethan. He remembered the Overseer's comment about wanting to show the twins something outside the city.

"Yes...it does," the pretty girl replied.

"Can you take us there?" Ethan worked to regain his full composure.

"Are you sure you're ready?" asked Delia.

They nodded in confirmation.

And so the three of them headed out of the town's protective walls, and followed it around to the opposite side of the city. There in a patch of fog, a graveyard rested on top of the ground. The twins had never seen a burial ground like this before. The stone structure looked like a giant chest of drawers. Up and down its sides were drawers with names carved into them. Delia led them around the far side of the great stone encasement to an inscription four rows from the bottom.

Earnest Lambent

Dear friend and explorer extraordinaire

G.R. 3437 – 3451

Chapter Nine
A Friendly Home

The twins spent many days reading and rereading their ancestor's journal. There were things for the Lambent siblings to consider within the pages of the chronicle that would guide them in their plans for reaching Gloam. They read that Earnest had thought to mark his path through the dark land with markers. Upon each wooden marker he placed a reflective cap that glowed when light shined on it. Earnest described how he had driven one of these stakes into the ground every few hundred feet, making it possible to find his way back to Maridia, if the need arose. In addition to discovering such practicalities as the markers, Ethan and Eisley spent a fair amount of time mulling over their ancestor's encounter with the mysterious Gloamer named Llebmac and the fateful assault of the Watchers. The only real commonality the twins could find between themselves and the dark dwellers was language. Earnest had conversed with Llebmac, yet he hadn't done so with the Watchers. It wasn't clear if the Watchers or Llebmac were human. None of the Gloamers had ever revealed themselves to the Glæmian. According to the old legend, Riley had brought back many of the Gloamers from the darkness and the only notable distinction in their appearance from that of the people of Glæm had been their stark pale skin – a fact that was very understandable due to the lack of light. They discussed these and many other things exhaustively while reading over the journal. Finally, Eisley had enough of the repetitive studies and ventured out into town.

Eisley parted from her brother on the third morning after their visit to Earnest's gravesite. She and Ethan had been served meals in their room because Ethan wanted to focus solely on the journal. This day, however, after finishing breakfast, Eisley left the stuffy bedroom and headed to get some much-needed fresh air. She managed to make it to the front door without seeing a soul but as she was closing the door behind herself, she heard Delia's voice behind her.

"Good morning. I was beginning to think that you and your brother had become a permanent fixture in the spare bedroom."

"Good morning to you as well," replied Eisley with a giggle. "It is nice to be out of that room."

"Will Ethan be joining you?" questioned Delia.

"I'm afraid he won't – at least not today anyways. He's still going over the journal," said Eisley.

Eisley had seen this side of Ethan many times. Throughout their childhood, Ethan had chosen to stay home for the purpose of studying one subject or another while Eisley had gone with her parents on errands into town or sometimes even beyond Luminae to other small settlements scattered along the roads. Ethan had always found the kind of education discovered in books to be superior to "real life education," as their father had called it – a form of learning that had always been more to Eisley's liking. She often wondered why her brother, as bright as he was, didn't understand the value of going into the world to watch, listen and take in the many things going on. Ethan had said, time and again, that almost anything worth understanding in life could be adequately gleaned from a book. In this matter the twins had agreed to disagree.

Eisley told Delia of her desire to see more of Maridia and so they set off together. Delia took Eisley to the tailor's shop, who'd made the new clothes Eisley was wearing. After viewing the beautiful dresses that hung on display, Eisley thanked Mr. Oleg, that being his name, for her outfit. As the two girls exited Mr. Oleg's shop, Eisley spotted Deerborn through the hustle and bustle of the townsfolk. He was heading toward what looked to be someone's home.

"Deerborn!" shouted Eisley.

Peering through the passerby's, his searching eyes found her.

"Hello child," said Deerborn, coming to greet Eisley. "It's good to see you again. How is Jukes treating you and your brother?"

"Very well, thank you," answered Eisley, beaming back at the man to whom she felt strangely connected. It was as if he were a member of her family.

"I have just returned home from my post," continued Deerborn. "Had I not been on duty I would have visited the two of you sooner."

"I'm not sure you would have found them," interrupted Delia, as she came to stand by Eisley. "They've been locked away for days reading Earnest Lambent's journal."

Deerborn took in Delia's words, pausing momentarily. Then he invited the girls into his home. Deerborn's wife was there and, according to him, she was eager to meet the twins. The girls were happy to accept the invitation and the three of them entered the door that Eisley had seen Deerborn approaching moments earlier.

"Abril," called Deerborn to his wife, placing his helmet and sword upon the kitchen table with a loud CLANG. "We have company, love."

"I'll be down in just a moment," came a light voice from somewhere above.

The home was small in comparison to the Overseer's. At the front door there was a narrow stairway leading up. To the left of the steps was the kitchen, furnished with a simple table and two wooden chairs. Eisley assumed Deerborn and his wife had no children by this. Beyond the table stood a small, stone fireplace with a crackling blaze deep within. Upon the glowing hearth hung a pot whose contents bubbled up over the edges. Past the kitchen, there was a modest sitting area with three wooden chairs and a knee-high table. It was from under this table that a small creature rocketed forward, heading straight for Eisley. The creature, who appeared to be a mix between a small dog and a potato, was diverted by the call of Deerborn. The animal changed course and leapt up into the air, landing in Deerborn's outstretched arms.

"What is that?" questioned Eisley.

"That happens to be a D'mune," came the friendly voice of a woman descending the staircase. "His name is Poudis," she continued. "And I'm Abril." The woman took Eisley's hand in her own and said, "Deerborn has told me about you and your brother meeting him in the forest. I am so sorry you had to see that side of my husband. He really doesn't seem like the soldier type once you get to know him better."

Eisley agreed completely with Abril. She had already seen the more caring side of Deerborn, and was having a difficult time recalling the ferociousness of their first meeting. This was made harder because the man now lay in the floor talking to the D'mune, which stood upon his chest fidgeting back and forth with excitement. Deerborn made little noises that didn't seem as if they should be coming from a full-grown man much less from the Captain of the Maridian Guard.

"See what I mean," said Abril, "he's more like a child sometimes."

Eisley giggled. She was beginning to feel a connection to Deerborn's wife as well. To make the whole scene even more hilarious, Deerborn let slip his pet name for the creature – Poudis Love. At this Eisley, Delia and Abril all began to laugh aloud.

"Where are my manners, please have a seat," said Abril, motioning to the two empty chairs at the kitchen table. "Would either of you like tea?"

"No thank you," replied the girls.

As Eisley and Delia seated themselves, Deerborn picked himself up off the floor and came over to kiss his wife on the cheek. Abril smiled and returned his greeting. "Ah, it's good to be home love," sighed Deerborn, running his fingers through Abril's golden locks. Eisley thought them to be very much in love. Then she heard a scurrying noise under the table. At her feet, the D'mune looked up at her with large, pleading eyes.

"Hello there," said Eisley, not convinced she really wanted to pick up the pitiful looking creature. She was sure, however, that her mother would have mistaken Poudis for a rat.

"It's alright," said Deerborn. "He wont hurt you. You can hold him if you'd like."

Eisley cautiously bent over to pick up the D'mune but Poudis bypassed her hands and leapt directly on to her lap. Eisley's startled look brought laughter to the room once again.

"You know, you're actually kind of cute, aren't you?" Eisley began to stroke the creature, who twittered and rolled over, evoking another round of giggles from the girls.

While petting the thing Eisley asked, "Where do D'munes come from? We don't have them in Glæm."

"They are indigenous to the mountain region," answered Abril. "They've never lived elsewhere as far as we know."

"In fact," added Deerborn, "it is believed that the D'mune have some strange connection to the mountains because they only live on the hills themselves and never in the wooded land below."

"There are many of them, then?" asked Eisley, now rubbing the creature's belly.

"Yes," answered Abril. "But not many are tame like Poudis here."

Eisley couldn't wait for her brother to see the creature. She wondered how Ethan was faring, alone in their room, and thought she should check on him soon. But she hadn't been surrounded by laughter and good cheer since her journey began, and she wasn't ready to leave her newfound friends just yet.

"Are you alright, child?" said Abril.

"I'm fine," said Eisley, shaking herself from thoughts of home. "I was just thinking about my brother."

"Where is he now?" asked Abril.

"He's at Jukes' house reading Earnest's journal," answered Eisley.

"He must find it very interesting," said Delia. "If I recall correctly, it isn't very long. How many times has he read it now?"

"We were on the fourth time through when I decided to leave," answered Eisley.

"Why does he continue to read it?" Deerborn asked.

"He is hoping it will help prepare us for Gloam," said Eisley.

"You can't be serious," exclaimed Delia, a worried look on her face. Abril and Deerborn mirrored her expression.

"You did read what happened to Earnest Lambent in Gloam didn't you?" asked Deerborn.

"Yes, we read it," answered Eisley. "However –" She paused, not sure how to best explain their motivations for moving forward. "Have you all heard of the Magic Lantern and the Boy of Legend?"

"I believe we are all familiar with Earnest Lambent's accounts of them, yes," answered Abril.

Eisley continued, "The Boy of Legend is our ancestor and we feel, in some way, obligated to follow in his footsteps. I can't explain it any better than that."

She had said it – obligated. No longer was this just the random adventures of two young siblings with no purpose in mind. After making the trek to Maridia, reading Earnest's journal, learning of his death at the hands of the Gloamers and seeing his gravesite, Eisley was certain that she and her brother were some how obligated to go to Gloam – come what may. She knew, despite their recent arguments, Ethan must feel the same way.

"Please," said Abril, "please reconsider child. It is folly to enter Gloam. We don't know enough about the wretched land to enter safely."

Abril's expression was similar to what Eisley might have expected her mother's face to look like at the thought of her daughter going into the darkness. Eisley wished she hadn't said anything about their plans.

"I'm sorry," said Eisley, "I cannot explain it except to say that we are being steered there."

"I'm, uh…" said Delia, stumbling over her words, "I just remembered I'm supposed to meet with my father for lunch. I need to go." Delia stood abruptly and walked toward the door. Then remembering her manners she turned and asked, "Would you like to come back with me?"

Eisley looked down at Poudis in her lap. He had fallen asleep on his back, four hairy little paws stretched upward.

Abril smiled. "Deerborn and I would be happy to have you stay here for a while. We'd love to hear more about your home and your family."

"I think I'll stay here a bit longer, then," said Eisley.

"Alright," replied Delia. "I'll see you this evening then... perhaps at dinner?"

"Yes, I'll see you then," answered Eisley. "Goodbye and thanks for the company."

Delia nodded awkwardly, then departed.

"Delia was acting a bit odd," said Abril. "Don't you think so, love?"

"Aye," said Deerborn. "That she was."

Abril did her best to steer the conversation away from talk of Gloam and succeeded. The rest of the afternoon was filled with many splendid discussions of family, love and, much to Eisley's delight, Glæm, its never darkening skies and the light that makes it that way. Though the afternoon was the best that she'd had since leaving home, Eisley couldn't help but notice the troubled look upon Deerborn's face that endured the afternoon through.

Chapter Ten
A Curious Invitation

Ethan looked up from Earnest's journal trying to focus his eyes on the room around him. He looked out the window and noticed that twilight would be upon him soon. Eisley had left him alone early that morning and hadn't yet returned. He felt certain that he'd covered all of Earnest's writings thoroughly. Ethan now knew Earnest's mind better than any living Lambent. On many issues, Ethan felt he and the long deceased Lambent agreed. Both felt awe at the amount of knowledge stored up in Maridia. From books stacked high in the library, to the university that Jukes had mentioned, Ethan felt their lure bidding him to remain in Maridia as Earnest had before him. Too, Earnest's final goal of reaching Gloam had always been in mind, even with his desire to stay in this town; in this Ethan felt the most like his ancestor.

He stood and walked to the bedroom window, facing east. There, in the distance was Gloam, reachable and even now so close and so deadly. Ethan thought back to his discussion with Jukes concerning Light as the Creator of everything. He wanted desperately to go to Gloam and see if there was any credence to this Maridian philosophy. He wasn't sure what he'd find but he was nearly certain that the answers lay there in the deep of night rather than in Maridia. But more than curiosity, which had always been his driving force, was the distinct feeling that he was being pulled towards the deadly land. It was as if his legs operated independently of his mind, and were determined to lead him into peril, willingly or not. However, he knew quite well that he was more than willing to continue on in this journey. Did his sister still want to move forward as she had a week ago? Or had the pages of the journal convinced her otherwise?

Ethan was startled from his thoughts by a knock at the door.

"Hello, there," said Alaric Jukes, stepping into the room. "Do you have everything you need? It has been days since we last spoke and I wanted to make sure you were being cared for properly."

"I'm fine, thank you," replied Ethan. "But have you seen my sister?"

"Yes, she's at Deerborn's house visiting with him and his wife," answered Jukes. "A lovely woman that Abril. Delia was there with them earlier." Jukes appeared to be pondering something. "Would you like to meet the rector of our university? He is usually free at this time of day and I have already made mention of you to him. He cannot wait to meet you, dear boy."

Ethan sat quietly for a moment deciding whether or not going to the university would affect his decision to go to Gloam.

"Well...what do you say, my boy? Shall we?" Jukes persisted.

Ethan thought getting out of this room might do him some good, so he agreed. However, he did find it a curious thing that he'd just been thinking about this very matter only moments ago.

Stepping out into the daylight, Ethan and Jukes made their way to the university. Crossing under the majestic entryway, Ethan read above him, THE WAY TO KNOWLEDGE, engraved in the marble. The two walked down a lantern lit marble hallway, each step echoing loudly. The Overseer stopped at a closed door, knocked once and entered a classroom filled with students. Ethan was surprised by the number of students here since he had been taught at home his whole life. He wondered if this class was taught by the rector, himself. But Jukes had said that he would be free this time of day…very curious.

As he stood there alone waiting for the Overseer to return, Ethan took in the grandeur of the facility. The only building in the entire town that was larger than the university was the home where Ethan and his sister stayed. And although Jukes' house might be slightly bigger, the university's architecture was doubtlessly grander. The walls of the school bore intricate carvings all throughout that must have represented the histories of Maridia. One carving next to Ethan depicted the city and its mountain, and on another hillock, a small town. In the valley between the settlements stood tiny soldiers locked in an epic battle. As he gazed intently at the handiwork of a master carver, Jukes stepped out of the classroom followed by a tall, lanky man in a long black robe with a matching black beard. The man stepped around Jukes in order to get a better look at Ethan.

"Ethan," said Jukes, "may I introduce you to Rector Osric."

"Good afternoon, young man," said the Rector. "I've heard so much about you."

"Hello," said Ethan, intimidated by the man's deep voice.

"Jukes tells me you are interested in our school," said the Rector. "I cannot tell you how much it would please me to instruct a Glæmian. In all my years of teaching I have never once had a student from your land. I have, myself, traveled into Glæm and visited your shining city of Awendela. I must say, it was quite impressive; however, by way of scholasticism your people seem to do themselves a great disservice."

"In what way?" questioned Ethan.

"There are too many ways to discuss here and now young man, though I'd say, in summation, the area in Glæmian thought that needs copious amounts of attention would be its philosophy department. Your kind are too narrow-minded."

"Ah, yes," said Jukes, proudly gripping the lapels of his coat, "Ethan and I have already had this discussion, haven't we lad?"

Ethan nodded, but said nothing. He began to see the chasm between his understanding of life and that of the Maridians. His better judgment told him to be wary of these new ideas, although he still held a great curiosity for this new way of thinking. He wished he could stay there for a time to better understand the views of the people. Had he already closed the door to that path completely?

A few things troubled Ethan – how had the Maridians been to Glæm without its inhabitants knowing? Also, thinking back now on the numerous Glæmian volumes in the Maridian library, Ethan wondered how these mountain dwellers had obtained all of that literature? Could it be that there were some Glæmians that knew of Maridia? Ethan, still feeling intimidated by the scholar, decided not to bring up the subject at present.

"If you decided to join us here," boomed the Rector, "you would have at your disposal some of the most learned minds in all the lands."

"Consider it, won't you, lad?" said Jukes.

"Come, Ethan let me show you around."

The afternoon seemed to end before it had begun. Ethan spent the latter part of the day in Rector Osric's office learning of the many courses available to him. As enjoyable as the afternoon had been, he had missed the company of his sister who presently entered their bedroom where Ethan now sat staring into the glowing fire. Eisley came to sit next to Ethan on his bed. Seeing her now, reminded him of how much they had been through together in such a short amount of time. He recalled the night they discovered the truth of Riley Lambent and the lantern. He remembered the look on Eisley's face as she stood in the clearing near their home, preparing to go into the unknown with him, lantern in hand. He remembered their travels, which ultimately led them here. Seeing her and being close to her somehow strengthened his resolve to submit to the mysterious summons that urged them toward Gloam. He felt that it was not his own will pulling him towards the darkness, but something outside himself.

Ethan smiled at his sister. "How was your day?"

"It was amazing!" exclaimed Eisley. "I spent the afternoon with Deerborn and his wife, Abril. She is wonderful company. She reminds me a little of Mother."

The mention of their mother brought a twinge of homesickness to Ethan, and he tried his best to push thoughts of his family from his mind. He knew how hurt they must be at his and his sister's disappearance. Grandpa Emmett was, Ethan knew, even now leading a search for them. Ethan was sure that his Grandpa believed he and his sister followed his directions, and, since they had not, it was unlikely that the Lambents would find their missing children.

"I wonder how they are," Eisley thought aloud. "I mean Mother and Father."

"Probably frantic," answered Ethan. "And rightfully so, I suppose. Have you thought much of turning around and going home?"

"Oddly enough...I've been thinking the opposite," stated Eisley. "I'm ready to go forward."

"Me too," said Ethan, looking down at the journal and the lantern that lay on the floor next to his bed. "I can't explain it but even as dangerous as it is probably going to be, I'm ready to face it."

"That's exactly how I feel," said Eisley. "Only..."

"What?" urged Ethan, placing his hand on his sister's shoulder.

"Well, I told Deerborn and Abril what we were planning to do and they practically begged me not to go. Then, for the rest of the afternoon, Deerborn had the most melancholy expression."

"I'm sure he was just thinking about what might happen to us," responded Ethan.

Eisley looked at him. "Have *you* thought about what might happen to us?"

"Yes." He paused. "And I also thought we should ask Deerborn to take us as far as the Eastern Lookout, near the border of Gloam. I was hoping he might teach us a few things about defending ourselves with a sword while we travel."

"Why don't we go to his home in the morning and talk to him about doing that?" said Eisley. "You need to meet Abril anyway, and that will give you a chance to do so before we go."

"So you're still sure about going?" asked Ethan.

"I'm ready," she answered determinedly.

Ethan wasn't sure what exactly drove them, but he knew he could trust his sister and the bond that had deepened between them in the previous weeks. Even if the road ahead was dark, the assurance of his sister's presence settled him. They would be together, no matter what happened.

The next morning the twins got up and, skipping breakfast altogether, headed straight for Deerborn's home. Abril was pleased to finally meet Ethan, and Deerborn was happy to see him again as well. Ethan shared his plan with Deerborn, asking his bearded friend to accompany them to the borderlands and train them to fight along the way. At this, Deerborn's expression changed. Like they had the day before,

Deerborn and Abril pled with the twins to stay away from Gloam. Deerborn even offered to escort Ethan and Eisley home, suggesting that he and his wife could stay with the Lambents for a while. Eisley's descriptions of Glæm had stirred the hearts of this couple.

But the idea of a journey into peril seemed out of the question to Deerborn. He denied their request for help outright, saying he couldn't bear to aid them in what would most certainly be their doom. Ethan and Eisley left shortly after Deerborn's stubborn refusal, feeling a bit aggravated as they went. They hated to leave Deerborn on shaky terms but they had no choice. Their departure from Maridia was drawing close, help or none.

Chapter Eleven
Something Unexpected

Alaric Jukes also disapproved of the twins' plan. The Overseer tried desperately to show them the imprudence, as he'd described it, in their goal. He recalled the murder of Earnest in great detail, to make his plea more dramatic. Jukes even went as far as to offer Ethan permanent lodging in his home along with an education from the university. In addition, he proffered to have Eisley escorted back to Luminae by Deerborn and his entire unit. Both of the twins wondered at the Overseer's motivation. Neither could decide if these overly hospitable proposals came from his desire to keep them safe, or if they came from the pleading of Delia who had been upset ever since her discovery of the twins' intentions or if they came from some other motivation entirely. Either way, the offer was turned down. Ethan found himself desiring to see more of Delia, a feeling that was intensified by the fact that she was visibly distraught by his coming departure. He wanted to comfort her in some way but he knew that what she wanted, namely for him to stay, could not happen now. Ethan asked Jukes if the offer for a Maridian education would still stand at a later date (provided, of course they returned from Gloam alive). Jukes tried to talk Ethan into staying yet again, but in the end he agreed. Ethan was glad for that glimmer of hope in an otherwise rather unforeseeable future.

It took the twins a few days to gather the supplies they would need to continue their journey. Eisley decided to take on the burden of another small pack in order to carry more food. This time they would bring some fruit, cheese and bread with things similar to the first leg of their adventure.

Ethan was not without his extra load either. For the next part of their journey, he would shoulder a bag full of wooden markers similar to those that Earnest had written about. Ethan had managed to find a reflective cloth to wrap around the markers in Mr. Oleg's textile shop. This would provide the luminescent effect needed in the dark land. All of these provisions where given to the twins by Jukes, who in the end, gave up fighting against their departure and revealed himself as a rather generous friend.

Finally the day came for the Lambents to leave Maridia. Unknown to them, Jukes had provided one more beneficial arrangement in the form of an escort named Deerborn. Their scruffy, red-headed friend asked if he could guide Ethan and Eisley at least as far as the Deadwood, which lay on the brink of Gloam. Deerborn and Abril had come to this decision collectively, knowing that they couldn't stand for the twins to go alone. Ethan couldn't imagine how the Captain of the Guard could take them to the edge of the darkness and leave them there.

Abril came to see her husband off, and was accompanied by the D'mune named Poudis, who was oblivious to the tension in the air. Poudis sprang into Deerborn's arms and the two had a brief, unintelligible conversation with one another.

Then Deerborn turned to his wife and embraced her passionately. All who were present wondered why the man would say his goodbyes to his wife in such a way. He had traveled to the Eastern Lookout, near the border, many times on patrol. While this embrace continued, Ethan bashfully turned his attention toward Alaric and Delia.

Delia's eyes were still red and puffy from crying earlier that morning. Eisley sympathized with Delia, knowing of her affection for Ethan. Ethan did something that Eisley had never seen her brother do before – with a determined stride, Ethan walked up to Delia and kissed her on the cheek. His and Delia's faces turned as red as the sky at sunset, and Ethan pretended not to see the look on the Overseer's face as he bid the flummoxed man farewell. Eisley hid a grin, amused both by her brother's boldness and his great embarrassment. The departing company finished saying their farewells and were off through Maridia's main gate.

The sky was clearer than normal, which made the entire mountaintop visible from the gate. The twins could clearly see their ancestor's grave around the bend in the city as the three travelers headed down the path toward the mountain lift that had carried them up to Maridia many days before. As they boarded the platform, Ethan marveled again at its construction and ingenuity. Then he asked, "Deerborn, why was this lift made? Wouldn't it have been a bit more practical to have just carved out a road into the side of the mountain?"

"Yes," said Deerborn. "It would have been a simpler way of doing things, had this been a normal mountain."

"What do you mean?" asked Eisley.

"Well," said Deerborn, "by normal, I mean if it had been made of a rock that is actually penetrable."

The twins looked perplexed so Deerborn clarified. "Not one mountain in all of this range is capable of being carved out by man. No one knows why really, though it never stopped people from inhabiting their heights. You see, we Maridians, like the other mountain dwellers, have tried for years to discover a way to blast into the hillsides. Surely you wondered why there was no water in the well in the center of town."

Ethan nodded.

"It's because we can't get to the water in the depths of the mountain."

"But then why was the fountain even built and, for that matter, where does the town's water come from?" asked Ethan

"We get our water from the base of the mountain. That is the main reason that the lift system was fashioned, though I know not why the fountain was built. Perhaps it was constructed in hope of there one day being a way to drill into the rock below."

"If the rock cannot be cut, then how was the town built? There must be a foundation," said Ethan.

"There is a foundation but it rests on feet and feet of sediment," answered Deerborn.

"It seems like a lot of trouble to build an entire town in those conditions," said Eisley.

"Yeah," agreed Ethan. "It does. Wouldn't it have been easier to build the town in the valley?"

"Easier – yes," answered Deerborn. "But would it have been safer? No. Remember, young ones, where you travel. The mountain's height is a necessity for protection in these parts should the darkness ever creep towards us. "

The lift came to rumbling halt at the bottom of the mountain.

At the stable ahead of them, two men were hitching up the same wagon that they'd arrived on. Ethan was glad to know they wouldn't be traveling in chains this time.

"Speaking of the danger you go to face, I have a gift for the two of you." Deerborn reached into his carryall and pulled out two long objects wrapped in a heavy cloth. He unraveled the bundle to reveal two sheathed swords.

"Ethan, I took your suggestion to heart," said Deerborn. "I have decided to train you both to defend yourselves. I took the liberty of having Maridia's blacksmith, Mikael Temujin, select these swords for you out of some of his more recent forgings."

The twins were speechless as their friend handed them their very own weapons. They unsheathed their swords to reveal brightly polished blades.

"Mikael," continued Deerborn, "is rather young but he's a highly skilled smith, so the Maridian Guard has conscripted him to be our weapons master. I gave him your approximate builds and he thought, as I do, that this style of blade would be most appropriate."

Ethan and Eisley could see why the black-smith had chosen this style of sword for them. The one sided blades were as light as a feather. The twins had never seen their equal. On the leather hilts, which were three fists in length (much longer than those made by the hilt-smiths of Glæm) was inscribed the phrase *Geong ond Boud*. The swords were named alike in recognition of Ethan and Eisley being twins. Seeing this Eisley asked, "What do these words mean?"

"It is from an ancient language that has survived for centuries. If translated it would say 'Young and Bold.' It is our custom to name the blades by the personalities of their owner. I thought this saying fit the two of you perfectly," answered Deerborn.

Tears stung Eisley's eyes. The words caught in her throat as she flung her arms around their friend and protector.

Ethan voiced his thanks, still examining the blade.

Deerborn smiled at the twins. "I'm glad you like them." Ethan peered at the sword strapped to Deerborn's back. "May I ask what your sword is called?"

"It is called *De Beran*," answered Deerborn. "It means 'The Bear.'"

Eisley laughed aloud at this news and wiped the last tears from her eyes. She remembered thinking the big, bushy-haired Deerborn looked like a bear when they first met. "And *I* would say that your sword's name fits you too."

Deerborn helped the twins strap the swords to their backs. Ethan considered it to be their first lesson. He wondered how many lessons they would have together during their short journey to the edge of Gloam.

"How long will it take us to get to the Eastern Lookout?" questioned Ethan as he and Eisley climbed into the wagon.

"By horse, it will take less than a day." Deerborn took the driver's seat at the front of the wagon. "But we will have to set up camp at least once and then there is the matter of the two of you traversing the Deadwood beyond the Eastern Lookout."

"Will the Deadwood be hard to cross?" Eisley could sense an uneasiness in Deerborn's tone.

"In the light of day, no." replied Deerborn. "But in the dark – well, that's another story. There are many fallen trees to cross over, dead trees – all the product of no light."

"How long will you stay with us?" pressed Eisley.

Deerborn did not answer. Eisley assumed the gallop of the horses had drowned her out.

"I don't think he heard you," said Ethan, speaking Eisley's thoughts.

"That's alright, I'll ask him again later," she shrugged.

It took no time at all for them to make their way around the bottom of the mountain by the wide road that had been cut out through the trees. On the other side of the mountain stretched a long treeless valley, nearly the mirrored image of the one that had brought them to Maridia. In fact, if not for the absence of the lift and stable, Ethan would have sworn that they were on the same side of the mountain they had just come from. The smooth road made for a pleasant ride although Deerborn was moving at a more leisurely pace than Ethan would have preferred. It was likely that Deerborn thought the twins would decide to return to town if given enough time. But Deerborn didn't know the mind of Ethan and that of his sister. If this is what the man hoped, he was gravely mistaken.

Instead of discouraging the twins, their view of the Eastern Lookout gave them a fresh excitement for what lay ahead. Ethan turned back toward the mountain they'd lodged on for the last week and looked towards the town that stood proudly above them. He could distinguish the part of the outer wall that made up Jukes' home and could even see the study window belonging to the Overseer on the fourth floor. He thought he could almost make out the silhouette of a man and girl staring out towards the small party as they traveled toward Gloam.

Chapter Twelve

The Blade, The Dream, The Darkness

The company had been traveling for hours when Ethan noticed a bridge ahead of them and a creek flowing under it. The stream seemed to noodle its way out of the forest on one side of the road and back into the wood on the opposite side. He wondered to himself if this was part of Luminae's Noodle Creek. When the three travelers arrived at the bridge, Deerborn veered from the road and proceeded towards the creek's bank. There he allowed the horse to drink.

"I think this is where we'll stop for the day," said Deerborn as he jumped down from the wagon.

Looking up towards the sky, Eisley asked, "Why? We have plenty of light to travel by."

"You're right. There is enough light to continue on a few more hours but if you plan to get in any training with that new weapon of yours, we're going to need to start soon."

"Not to mention we won't use up our own water supply if we stop by a creek," Ethan was petting the horse by the water's edge.

"Precisely why I stopped here, young one," said Deerborn. "You do have a keen mind don't you?"

The party set up camp and gathered firewood from the nearby forest. After they had all their provisions, Deerborn bade the twins to unsheathe their swords.

"Alright," he began. "We are going to start with the fundamentals. First you need to know your weapon." Deerborn held up his sword. "The handle is called the hilt. You will notice that my sword has a cap on the end of the hilt. This is called a pommel."

"Why do our swords look so different from yours?" asked Ethan. Deerborn's sword looked similar to those that his grandfather made.

"Well, I guess we could start there couldn't we? Our swords are different because they facilitate two completely different styles of fighting. I use an older style, which was once known the world over. The old style is more brutal and requires more strength than skill. However, through the centuries the Maridians have developed a new style of combat which is much more elegant. As such, the newer style, called Protegere, brought with it a need for a longer and lighter weapon."

Deerborn asked Ethan for his sword so that he could compare it to his own. He held them up together. "See the difference?"

Ethan and Eisley appreciated the stark contrast between the two. Their swords were nearly twice as long, both the blade and the hilt. Where Deerborn's blade was wide, theirs were thin. As for the difference in the hilts, Deerborn's was designed for one-handed combat where the twin's appeared to be made for two hands. Deerborn returned Ethan's sword and continued their lesson.

"This is the cross guard," said Deerborn, pointing to the piece that divided the blade from the hilt. "And, obviously, this," he said pointing to the sharp, shining metal, "is called the blade. You will also notice that my blade is double-edged while yours has a single edge. This may not seem like a big difference now, but when you learn to block with your sword you will see where you have leverage that I do not have." Deerborn pretended to cut himself while holding one side of his blade as if to use it to block an oncoming blow. He cracked a wide smile and said, "And you will both need the extra leverage much more than I would."

"Because you are bigger and stronger," said Eisley.

"Exactly dear," answered Deerborn. "You seem to be getting the idea, Eisley."

"Our grandfather has a forgery," she replied. "So we probably know a little more about swords than the typical Glæmian."

"Is that so?" questioned Deerborn. "What need would your people have of sword-smiths? I thought your kind lived in peace."

"We do, but our grandfather wanted to keep the old art of sword-making alive," replied Ethan. "There was a time when our people where not much different than Maridians."

Deerborn grumbled. "I would have never thought there would be a forgery in Glæm."

"Oh, there's more than one," said Eisley. "Grandpa has many friends who assist him in the work."

"Wonders never cease," replied Deerborn. "Now back to our lesson. Though I wonder now if you already know the things I'm teaching you?"

Ethan answered that he knew a good bit about the parts of a sword but his sister didn't because she hadn't spent as much time in their grandfather's smithy as he had.

"Well, then." Deerborn spoke more to Eisley than Ethan. "The next thing you need to know is how to hold your swords. Your hilt is long, and for a good reason. Place one hand at the bottom of the grip and the other at the top, leaving a fist's length between the two. This will give you more balance and control over your weapon."

The twins positioned their hands as Deerborn had instructed and then listened as he began to explain the basics of blocking. They learned that the core of this new style was defending oneself against an enemy rather than provoking an attack, whereas the older form had been designed with an offensive approach in mind. "The Maridians once held a 'conquer and destroy' mentality," Deerborn told them. "In time, this mind set was replaced with a new one – 'defend and protect.'" Both twins thought the newer approach was much more pleasant.

"Why would one people ever want to take another's lands?" questioned Eisley. "That seems very selfish."

"Indeed it does," said Deerborn. "But I'm afraid it isn't always that simple, dear one."

"Well, it should be," said Ethan. "Let's say, for instance, that Maridians weren't happy with only the mountain they had. What justifiable reason would they have to take over other mountain towns? Like Farthenly, for instance."

"Farthenly?" said Deerborn. "What do you know of Farthenly?"

"Our grandmother is from there," answered Eisley. "We learned this only days before you found us."

"Farthenly was the last town conquered under our old system," said Deerborn.

Both Ethan's and Eisley's expressions changed to concern.

"Oh don't worry," said Deerborn quickly. "This was over a century and half ago. We eventually relinquished our rule over conquered territories under the new governmental system, established by the ancestors of Alaric Jukes. When the old ways were abolished, the people of Farthenly began to rule themselves again. Though once they were free, they started to shrink in numbers."

"Why?" asked Ethan.

"Many of the people who lived there relied heavily on Maridia's governing and economy and moved to the citadel under the new and much improved rule of the Jukes family."

"Maridia must have been much larger in those days," said Ethan.

"Yes, it was," answered Deerborn, solemnly. "It took many generation to dwindle to the size it is now but eventually people moved or families died off. There are some who blame the Jukes for the decrease in population. They claim the new system disturbed the flow of trade and commerce, though I believe the Jukes' did the right thing by allowing those in bondage to regain their freedoms. I often wonder if there has ever been another civilization to give up its conquered lands for moral reasons, such as Maridia did."

"Does your library tell of none?" asked Ethan.

"None," said the man.

Ethan thought back to the carvings on the walls in the university hallways and wondered if the one he'd seen depicted the battle between Maridia and Farthenly.

"Lets get to work then," said Deerborn bringing Ethan out of his reverie and back to the training at hand.

The few remaining hours of daylight were spent learning different sorts of defensive moves. After nightfall, which came a little sooner than the twins had expected, the company lit a fire and as they sat around it they ate and talked of many things, some trivial and some serious. What surprised Ethan the most was how Deerborn always seemed to steer the conversation back towards the subject of Glæm. He wondered why the man would be so interested in Glæm, having such an incredible life already. Though, what he began to notice was that Deerborn's curiosity wasn't for Glæm at all but rather the Light of Glæm. Eisley also had more to say about the light than Ethan thought she would. She spoke of the light with such joy and passion. It reminded him of the way he would linger on other subjects. Oddly enough, he found himself yearning, just as Deerborn seemed to, for her understanding of the Glæmian Light. It was as if Ethan was beginning to grasp the depth of what had surrounded him his whole life. Certainly his parents had lived by precepts of the Light their whole life, and had instilled these ways deep within him and his sister. Yet Ethan had never felt as connected to the Light as his sister had and this always puzzled him.

That night Ethan dreamed more vividly than he could ever remember. In his dreams the wall carvings from the university in Maridia had sprung to life. He saw himself and Eisley there surrounded by soldiers, all of whom battled furiously against a shadowy, hidden foe. He saw Deerborn, and to his great surprise he spotted his family, all of them moving in to surround the twins in the heat of battle. Then his dream quickly changed direction.

A vision appeared of a metal emblem that resembled Riley's lantern in shape but with a circle surrounding it. The emblem was spinning, slow at first but then faster and faster. Suddenly it changed shape, and he stood before an object too bright to make out at first. After his eyes had adjusted to the brilliant glow Ethan realized it was the Magic Lantern. The Lambent heirloom appeared to be floating of its own accord.

When dawn arrived, Ethan couldn't get the images from the dream out of his mind. He questioned his sister and Deerborn about the emblem he'd seen in his dream, and neither had the slightest clue as to what it might mean. The company ate a quick breakfast and then went over the things they had learned in their training the night before. Much to Deerborn's delight the twins had retained all that he taught them. He told them to continue to process what they learned throughout the day and promised that there would be more to learn that evening when they reached the Eastern Lookout. And reach it they did, with plenty of daylight left to spare.

The three travelers left the horse tied to a feeding station at the base of the mountain and then traversed the side of the mountain on foot. Deerborn apologized to the twins for the inconvenience of the climb, explaining that they hadn't seen the need in building a lift like the one in Maridia just for the soldiers, who were the only ones to travel to the lookout.

When they reached the top, the guards on duty greeted the trio. The lookout was small compared to what they had seen in Maridia, just a simple round, wooden, two-story structure. The upper floor had no walls, only a roof, and looked similar to a pavilion on a large platform. They entered the lookout and Ethan saw nothing more than a few cots for sleeping, a table, a small armory, and a pit in the center of the room with a tiny fire burning in it. Ethan looked up to see a round whole in the room directly above fire pit. A ladder leaned against the far wall, and was the only way to access the lookout above.

"Come, have a look," said Deerborn, who was already climbing the ladder.

The twins followed him onto the upper level. When they reached the top, Ethan and Eisley gasped at what they saw. Miles of decaying forest stretched out before them, making up the Deadwood, and beyond that, only blackness. The clouds were so dark and reached so far in every direction on the horizon that there was nothing else to be seen. Not even the sky. It was as if the clouds swallowed the sun and wanted to devour all the remaining good in the world.

Deerborn took note of the twins' response to what they saw. "Everyone reacts as you do, the first time they see it this closely."

Neither sibling spoke. They could only look out toward their destination, the thing that could bring the utter ruin of all.

At the first sight of Gloam, Ethan and Eisley grew much more serious about their training. The rest of that day was spent in the upper level of the lookout revisiting the fighting techniques that the twins had already learned. The siblings decided, with recommendations from Deerborn, that they should stay at the lookout and continue their defensive education for a few more days, at the very least. Once the night's exercises ended, Deerborn brought the twins downstairs into the soldiers' quarters for a dinner of cheese and bread. The meal was well received, as were the cots that brought much needed sleep. Ethan and Eisley were both grateful to the two guards, Blaise and Watts, who had gladly given up their cots and slept on the ground so that the twins could rest more comfortably.

A guard doesn't sleep much, as the twins learned early the next morning. Ethan woke to the sound of Watts humming a sacred sounding tune on the platform above them. Once he had come to his senses, he realized that Deerborn was already awake and laughing above as well. Eisley heard the laughter and sat up slowly on her cot. "I feel like we just went to sleep."

"Yeah," yawned Ethan, "me too."

The two sat quietly listening to the muddled conversation above them for a few moments and then Eisley broke the silence.

"Do you think we will be able to do this...I mean go into Gloam?" she questioned.

"Yes," assured Ethan.

"What about the swords?" said Eisley, "Do you think we'll have to use them?"

"I'm not sure," replied Ethan, "I hope not. With the lantern, I don't think any Gloamers would get close enough to us for us to even use the swords."

"Do you think they use swords in Gloam?" asked Eisley.

"I'm not sure," began Ethan. "The only weapon that Earnest wrote about was the darts. Speaking of that, I've decided to ask Deerborn if he has any extra armor."

"I think that's a great idea," answered Eisley, who stood to her feet and stretched.

"Do you really think the Captain of the Guard hadn't thought of that already?" Deerborn's voice carried from the top of the ladder. He had stuck his head through the passage to check on the twins, and overheard the last part of their conversation. "Once you're ready, come join me up here."

The twins climbed up on the platform where they found Deerborn huddled in conversation with Blaise and Watts leaning against a post singing. Watts tipped his hat toward the siblings never skipping a beat in his tune.

"Good morning," said Deerborn. "A bit sore are we?" he added noticing their stiff movement.

They nodded. Ethan was surprised to see that Eisley was as sore as him.

"Your aching will go away soon enough," smiled Deerborn. After a moment his expression darkened. "But, your continued desire to go into that forsaken land baffles me. I do not pretend to understand your reasons; however, I see that you will not be swayed in your decision. My last hope of seeing you change your mind was diminished last night when you continued to train even after seeing Gloam."

"Blaise," said Deerborn, motioning to the guard. "Go and retrieve two sets of the Protegere armor."

"Yes sir," said the soldier.

The guard retreated down the ladder and reappeared a few moments later carrying two sets of the silly looking wooden armor that most of the soldiers wore in Maridia. The twins recalled the first time they'd seen the soldiers wearing it the night they'd been taken captive by Deerborn.

"I thought I would give you this armor if the occasion ever actually called for it," said Deerborn. "I believe it is calling presently."

Blaise handed the armor over to Deerborn who held it out before the twins. "This is Protegere armor," he said. "It was created to compliment the Protegere fighting style."

"I noticed the difference in yours and your men's armor the first day we met," said Ethan to Deerborn. "But I thought the difference had to do with rank. Is your armor for the old fighting style then?"

"Yes," said Deerborn. "As with my sword, you must have brawn to use my armor because it's much heavier. Protegere is much more efficient in keeping your enemy from getting near you, so the need for heavier armor all but disappears...along with the use of older combative methods. Now, as for what I overheard you speaking about downstairs. If the Gloamers still use darts, this armor won't protect you completely, though I dare say it will guard you better than nothing at all."

Deerborn laid the armor down and asked the twins if they were ready to continue in their training. Immediately the twins could tell that the training would take on an entirely new dynamic with the new day. Rather than learning the techniques individually, as they had thus far, Deerborn gave them wooden swords that were to be used for sparring. They were to apply what they had learned in previous days. The passing morning brought with it many revelations concerning the art of wielding a blade, such as how hard it is to implement memorized defensive methods in the heat of combat. As hard as the sparring had seemed that morning, it was made even more difficult when Deerborn bade the twins to don their armor to get accustomed to fighting with the cumbersome extra weight.

Deerborn sparred some with Ethan and Eisley, but more often than not he relegated this task to Blaise and Watts who where much more fluent in the new style than himself. Deerborn explained that all Maridian soldiers were taught Protegere, but some, like himself, desired to learn the older style as well. Soldiers who learned the old methods usually decided to stay with that style because it was fresher in their minds by that point.

By sundown the twins were exhausted and ready once again for sleep. Deerborn told them how pleased he was with their progress, but advised that they spend a few more days learning sword-craft before moving forward with their journey. Even as sore as the Lambents were, they couldn't have agreed more with their friend.

Chapter Thirteen
Deadwood

Many days passed before Ethan and Eisley were ready to continue traveling eastward. They spent most of their time training, though Ethan had also requested instructions from Deerborn about how to survive the Deadwood. Maridian scouts had ventured into the wood from time to time, so Deerborn allowed the twins to pore over maps of the area surrounding the lookout. Their studies swallowed up each evening of their week at the lookout. Deerborn's mood darkened with every passing day, and it became very apparent that he was troubled by the idea of the twins' departure. Something changed in the man on the morning before they planned to leave. The Lambents saw Deerborn writing a letter that was given to Watts who headed west towards Maridia, singing as he went. They noticed a change in their friend's countenance from sorrow to determination. Ethan and Eisley speculated about the possible contents of the letter. They began to hope that Deerborn would decide to join them on their march into the Deadwood, although neither one dared to ask him about it. He had already done so much.

The morning of their departure finally arrived. Ethan felt more nervous than he ever had before. It must have been apparent to Eisley because she said to him, "Don't look so worried."

"I guess I am a bit nervous," responded Ethan, embarrassed by his inability to cloak his mood. "More than anything, I can't shake the feeling that I have somehow dragged you into this whole mess."

"I decided to join you on this little journey, Ethan. Remember?"

"Yes," said Ethan. "I remember. But it doesn't change the fact of the matter."

"And what is the fact of the matter?" asked Eisley.

"That, you are my sister and if anything happens to you, I..." Ethan couldn't finish because he didn't know what to say. Eisley had been in his life since day one and the thought of a decision that he'd made altering her life for the worse terrified him far more than even Gloam did.

"I have had plenty of chances to turn around," said Eisley. "I'm not leaving your side. Do you honestly think I feel any different than you? I'm afraid for you too. I'm afraid for us both."

Deerborn came up behind them and interrupted their conversation. "And *I'm* afraid that you two might have less to worry about than you think."

The twins turned to look at him.

"I am going with you."

Ethan sighed and Eisley smiled.

"I won't allow you to go into darkness alone," said Deerborn.

"What about your wife?" asked Eisley. "What would she do if something happened to you?"

"Dear one, Abril and I came to this decision together before we ever left Maridia. She feared for your safety as much as I do."

Ethan and Eisley stood before their selfless guardian, at a loss for words.

"The truth is, Abril and I consider you to be...family – even after knowing you for such a short time. We were never able to have children of our own." The man looked away to hide tears from a past pain rekindled. "I know you have parents that you love very much, and we would never assume to take their place..."

"I think we understand," said Ethan, looking to his sister to affirm his statement. "You have become a good friend to us. Thank you!"

Eisley couldn't speak. Tears welled up in her eyes as well. She wrapped her arms around Deerborn.

With a new vigor the twins gathered their things together. The trio descended the last of the Camel Back Mountains, and disappeared into the thick foliage below.

The greenery turned to a dead gray more quickly than either sibling anticipated. Within a few fleeting hours the party pushed through one last wall of living undergrowth and were faced with a sea of decaying trees. Ethan looked toward the sky to see that, even outside of the darkening canopy of trees where they just came from, the near night remained. Standing there, he knew even the twilight would soon fade to total darkness.

The Deadwood would be their greatest obstacle. As far as the eye could see, trunk after rotting trunk lay toppled over one another, reminding Ethan of a colossal bonfire awaiting its flame.

"Where do we begin?" questioned Eisley.

"Any place is as good as the next I suppose," answered Deerborn. "You saw for yourselves on the map that there is no real passage through the Deadwood. We need only to continue eastward in whatever way possible."

"I hope we are able to get across," said Eisley.

"Oh...don't worry young one, we'll make it across," said Deerborn. "Though, I wager it will be the most difficult march that any of us has ever had to make."

"Yeah," agreed Ethan, gazing toward the Deadwood in a trance.

At that moment, the sun broke through the clouds behind them, far to the west where it sat in the sky near the tops of the mountains. The sun shone on the Deadwood before them. A beam of sunlight rested on an entrance into the maze of fallen trees just south of where they stood. "Look," said Ethan, pointing towards the opening.

"Well," said Deerborn with a sigh, "we'd better get moving. The sun doesn't show its face very often in these parts so I'll take it as a sign."

A few hours later, and less than half a Glæmian mile into the Deadwood, the travelers decided to make camp. Winding around, through, over and under the fallen trees had proven to be exhausting. In no time at all, the trio had set up their tents and were sitting in front of a small, crackling fire. For the first time since leaving the Eastern Lookout, Ethan and Eisley noticed how quiet their surroundings were. There wasn't a noise to be heard anywhere save from the fire.

"Does anything live here?" said Ethan, breaking the silence.

"Nothing worth noting," answered Deerborn. "Only very small, very shy animals that will go out of their way to never make contact with us."

"Ethan, turn on the lantern and see if the animals sing," said Eisley.

Ethan grabbed the family heirloom while Eisley addressed the confusion on Deerborn's face. She told Deerborn of the curious draw that animals and insects alike had to the lantern when it was burning. As Deerborn pondered this, Ethan ignited the lantern and even with its brilliant light all remained silent. Though neither sibling spoke of it, the silence planted an ominous seed in their hearts that only grew from that point forward. As strange as the occurrence of the singing animals had been earlier in their travels, it brought a sense of hope with it. Now, in the silence of the dead forest, hope faded quickly.

The Lambents and Deerborn sat quietly in the heavy stillness until Eisley felt she had to say something. She couldn't think of a better way than asking about the contents of the letter Deerborn had sent with the soldier Watts the previous day.

"Deerborn," said Eisley, looking at the man who seemed deep in thought. "Can I ask you something?"

"Anything," answered the bearded man, peacefully.

"Were you sending Abril a letter yesterday?"

Deerborn grinned. "Yes I was. I was telling my wife that you two had not changed your minds and so I was going with you." He looked to Ethan as well. "I was also telling her that I would see her soon enough. That is, after your work is complete."

"Work?" questioned Ethan, "What do you mean?"

"I'm not sure," said Deerborn. "That was probably a poor choice of words. The two of you just seem so focused on reaching Gloam that it appears as if you have an unstated purpose for going."

Ethan could understand why Deerborn would think this. He thought it himself. He reflected on Riley Lambent and what he had accomplished while in Gloam, bringing all those Gloamers out of the darkness and into the Light of Glæm. Riley's adventurous spirit had been what spurred his own desire to leave home. Maybe they would complete some sort of work in Gloam. Although, the idea of retrieving a small crowd of Gloamers from the dark land now seemed minuscule in comparison to the immensity of the thing that drew him and his sister towards Gloam.

"You are right though," Deerborn smiled. "I was writing to my Abril."

Deerborn peered towards the black sky contemplatively. "We'd better get some rest. Tomorrow will be a day much like this one."

Deerborn's last words of the previous night proved to be very true. The trio's day (if you could call it a day with the waning light) was spent bobbing and weaving through a vast expanse of dead trees. As they made their way closer to Gloam, the twins recognized an element of the wood that they had not taken into account yet – the weather. The air grew increasingly colder with every step toward Gloam. Ethan ridiculed himself for not having thought of such a simple thing. Of course the lack of sunlight would mean colder air. What puzzled him the most was that Earnest had not mentioned this subject in the whole of his journal. Perhaps Earnest had traveled in a warmer season. It was true that winter was drawing near. Ethan wondered how long it would be before freezing weather came to settle on Gloam. It would surely be much sooner than in Luminae.

When they stopped to rest, the twins were relieved to find that Deerborn had anticipated the cold; he drew from his pack two gray soldier issued, coats with hoods. They were the perfect size for the twins.

"I thought these might come in handy," he said and handed the coats to the twins. He pulled out a coat of his own that matched Ethan and Eisley's.

How had Deerborn's bag held all three coats and everything else he carried? It must have been a talent acquired from years in the Maridian service, making treks of this nature on many occasions.

After a short rest the trio continued. The sky above gradually blackened as they traveled on, and the time came for them to light the lantern. Once again, and much to the twins' bewilderment, Deerborn pulled from the endless depths of his carryall a lantern that was slightly smaller than the Lambents'. He lit the lantern to add to the light already coming from Riley's. The twins noticed two things about Deerborn's lantern that differed from their own. The light from Deerborn's projected in a soft, steady glow, while Riley's projected bright, dancing streams of light. Deerborn also had to light his lantern with a piece of flint. The twins had only to turn a knob.

"Different make and model?" questioned Ethan.

"Or magic," said Eisley teasingly.

In their second day of traversing the Deadwood, the travelers fell into a rhythm that helped them to cross the miles of extreme terrain more easily. Deerborn guessed that they had nearly tripled their distance from the day before. A few hours and bruises later, Deerborn stopped in his tracks, startling the twins. They had become oblivious to their surroundings - partly because of the length of the trip, and partly due to the howling wind that had been gaining momentum throughout the day. The wind blew directly into their faces, making it nearly impossible to see or hear one another.

"Stay here for a few minutes." shouted Deerborn over the wind. "I'm going to go ahead and do a little scouting."

With that Deerborn was off. Eisley was sure the man had slipped into combat mode, which worried her.

"Scouting?" yelled Ethan. "He hasn't wanted to do that yet. I wonder what's going on?"

Eisley shrugged, intent on watching for Deerborn's return. Minutes later the friend-soldier returned.

"There is something I think you should see before we set up camp," said Deerborn as he motioned for Ethan and Eisley to follow him. Not far from where they had been standing the Deadwood forest came to an abrupt end. What the Lambents saw before them, illuminated only by the light of the lanterns, was a desolated flatland that appeared as though they stood on the brink of a great dark precipice. They had reached the edge of Gloam.

Deerborn stirred the twins from their stupor. "We need to go back into the cover of the Deadwood for the night. After sleep, we will continue."

The company made their way back to where the twins waited on Deerborn earlier. There, they set up camp and decided that it would be foolish to light a fire among the dead trees while the wind was blowing so strongly. They took shelter in their tents and used their lanterns as a source of warmth. The scene from the rim of Gloam pushed its way into Ethan and Eisley's dreams that night, causing their already growing fear of the unknown to settle in deeply.

Chapter Fourteen
Gloam

Deerborn awakened Ethan and Eisley in what appeared to be the middle of the night.

Disoriented, Ethan said, "Is...Is it morning?"

"I'm afraid so. The sun is gone. You two need to put your armor on before we go any further." Deerborn rose to walk away from the twins' tent, carrying his lantern to light the way back to his own shelter.

The wind blew so hard that the Lambents decided to put on their armor inside the tent to shelter themselves from the cold a little longer. Putting on armor in the confines of a tent was somewhat of an ordeal. There wasn't much room for maneuvering to begin with, and knees and elbows and foreheads bumped and knocked into each other. Ethan and Eisley said things to one another like, "Pull on that strap, would ya?" And, "I'm not sure I'm doing this correctly." When all was said and done the twins managed to don armor, coats, carryalls and swords.

"This should make traveling a bit easier," teased Ethan.

"Well at least we didn't have to wear all of this in the Deadwood," said Eisley.

"No...now we're just wearing the deadwood," laughed Ethan, pointing at the wooden armor and trying hard to make light of their situation.

After breaking down camp and attaching a few more odds and ends to their already substantial loads, the twins followed Deerborn back towards the border between the Deadwood and Gloam with apprehension in every step. Soon they stood in silence trying to make out anything in the impenetrable darkness.

"Where to?" Deerborn was as much at a loss of where to begin as the twins. No Maridian had traveled past the edge of the Deadwood.

Ethan and Eisley looked at one another questioningly. Then, pointing directly in front of him Ethan said, "This way." Ethan stepped out and the others followed.

By the light of the lanterns the trio saw that they were on an open plain that stretched out endlessly before them, which accounted for the severity of the wind. Ethan struggled to put one foot in front of the other, not sure whether this was due to the gale or the foreboding feeling in the pit of his stomach.

After an hour of unchanging conditions, the travelers noticed a flaky substance on the ground that hadn't been there earlier. Ethan was sure that this was the substance Earnest had written about in his journal. He stopped and bent down to retrieve a piece. The sample was light and also fragile. Ethan pressed it and it crumbled into pieces. Ethan blew the crushed matter from his palm and it took flight in the wind.

Eisley and Deerborn followed suit and bent to pick up their own specimens.

"I wonder what this stuff is?" questioned Eisley, holding it close to her face for better observation.

"I'm not sure," said Ethan. "I don't think I've ever seen anything like it before."

"Nor have I," said Deerborn, puzzled. "But it's everywhere."

Indeed the substance covered the ground, and with every step the travelers took it crunched beneath their feet. As the company pushed forward, hour after grueling hour, they noticed that the flaky matter began to disappear. They weren't sure if it was dissolving or if they had simply moved beyond the point where the substance grew. Though how it might grow no one could surmise because it wasn't attached to the ground. According to Earnest's findings, the flakes returned at roughly the same time every day. If this were true Ethan knew he'd be thankful for it because this would be his only indicator of time in Gloam.

As they traveled, Deerborn drove the reflective stakes into the ground every few hundred yards or so to mark their way home when needed, just as Earnest had on his journey. A small case of paranoia seized Deerborn, and he insisted on backtracking to assure that their markers where still in place. He felt certain that someone was following them. He said that a clever enemy might try to sabotage them by pulling up their stakes in an effort to trap them in the darkness. Still, every time they backtracked, the stakes were still in place. Ethan didn't think they would be able to hear anyone tracking them over the wind, which blew so that the travelers finally had to cover the entirety of the their faces with their hoods, leaving only a small hole for seeing what little they *could* see. This precaution kept them from being overly blistered by the gale. When they decided to sleep, the wind made it absurdly difficult to erect their tents. However, they finally completed the task and retreated into the makeshift protection of their portable residences. The twins decided to sleep in their armor so as to not repeat the events from early that day.

The night was uneventful, which gave the company a bit of solace in an otherwise anxious situation. The wind subsided into more of breeze during the night, but even then Ethan couldn't help but think that this was nothing more than the calm before the storm.

Ethan wondered where they were going. All he knew for sure was that the impulse to continue into Gloam hadn't gone away upon entering it. He was still being pulled, as it were, towards something that they hadn't reached. It was unexplainable other than to say that he knew they hadn't reached their final destination. He and Eisley knew their destinies lay in the direction that they traveled.

Soon after their second day in Gloam began, the trio noticed the flakes on the ground once more. As before, the flakes disappeared while they progressed forward.

The company continued on in the darkness, heading eastward to an unknown end. It became apparent to Deerborn that they would soon run out of markers. He suggested the possibility of turning around and heading back towards the Eastern Lookout. So far, they hadn't met anyone or anything, and there hadn't even been a change in the landscape. The Lambents adamantly refused this plan despite Deerborn's warning that they might not find their way out without markers. They were willing to take that chance, frightful as it was.

Fear built, wearying the travelers as the day progressed. They all wondered what would happen if the lantern's light died away, knowing the markers wouldn't matter if there was no light to find them. The darkness surrounding them was so absolute that all three considered the loss of their sanity if they were left without their source of light. Still they pressed on, subduing their fears. Ethan and Eisley focused on the feeling that compelled them forward, and Deerborn on his intense desire to protect the twins.

Once or twice Deerborn considered snatching up the siblings and sprinting toward home. He knew, however, that if he were to do this he would have to put them down sooner or later and they would take off again in the opposite direction. Ethan and Eisley would stay in Gloam with or without him. With the twins fixed on continuing forward, Deerborn had called them stubborn more than once, urging them to see reason. While it was true that the man understood the determination of a solider to continue forward in his duty, he couldn't wrap his mind around the Lambent twins' willingness to keep going on in a lightless country. Still, he cared for them dearly and because of this he knew that whatever compelled them, it had brought them a long way from home even before he had entered their journey. More than once, Ethan and Eisley suggested that Deerborn turn back toward Maridia and go home to Abril. They were sure

Deerborn would not leave their side, but they also knew this was not his task. His devotion to them drew the twins closer to their protector and friend.

After another day's travel, the trio camped again with much less trouble than the previous night. With the wind at a near standstill, the travelers decided to sit outside their tents and enjoy each another's company over the final meal of the day. They were tired of the dried meat and nuts, but were thankful for the food all the same.

Sleep danced on the edges of their minds when Deerborn first heard the noise. He didn't alarm the twins but suggested that they all retreat to their tents for the night. After Ethan and Eisley were fast asleep, Deerborn exited his own tent in the darkness and sat in the center of their camp, listening and waiting. He knew that there was someone or something close – very close. He could hear its short breath not far from their campsite. Deerborn wasn't sure if the intruder was simply an animal investigating the newcomers or something more. As he remained still, controlling the sound of his breathing, the prowler drew closer. He could hear it edging its way up the side of the twins' tent, moving to the entrance.

Ethan woke suddenly, hearing something. He moved quietly to grab his sword and the lantern and turned back toward the doorway. Ethan positioned himself between the entrance of the tent and his sister in case he needed to protect her from some unseen foe. Whatever it was sounded big. Ethan mustered his courage and ignited the lantern. A few things happened all at once. He twisted the knob on the lantern, which brought a blinding light into the closed quarters around him. He was face to face with some sort of wolf-like creature with a large mass of black matted fur and giant protruding fangs. The creature screamed at the sudden burst of light and stood up onto its hind legs to retreat from the source of its agony. As it did, the whole tent broke loose from the ground and lifted into the air with the monster. There it stood howling, trying its best to remove the tent from around its face with its front paws. Eisley screamed, awoken by the creature's howl. Ethan held his sword ready to do what he could to bring down the beast when suddenly it stopped howling. It stood for a second, swaying back and forth before diving directly towards the twins. Instinct took over as Ethan raised his sword towards the creature that came hard and fast toward him. With blade facing upward the monster dropped directly onto it, wrenching the sword from Ethan's hand in the process. The creature hit the ground then convulsed violently for a moment before breathing its last.

"Children!" screamed Deerborn, "Are you alright?"

Eisley was still screaming.

"I...I think we're okay," said Ethan, shaking and gasping for breath as he held tightly to his sister. "It's alright, Eisley girl," said Ethan trying to console her. "It's over...shh...shh. It's alright." Ethan wasn't sure he believed his own words. He too was scared, but found self control in calming his sister.

The tent that had been Ethan and Eisley's was now wrapped around the beast that lay dead before them. Deerborn surveyed the scene. He reached to pick up Riley's lantern, which Ethan had dropped in the commotion. It lay on its side, the light circling furiously within and projecting beams high into the clouds above. Then the ground shook uncontrollably below them, which only added to the hysteria of the moment. The shaking brought Deerborn to his knees. Once the earthquake was over, Deerborn stood and retrieved the light. He brought it close to the covered head of the creature where Ethan's sword had driven cleanly through its maw, exiting out the top of its head.

"Well met," said Deerborn, amused. Though how he was anything but frightened in this moment was hard to understand.

The man pulled the sword from the monster, causing a gurgling noise as it slid through. Ethan felt sick. Deerborn wiped the blade and handed it back to Ethan who, though nauseous, took the sword and sheathed it.

"Remember, always clean your blade after battle," said Deerborn in a soldierly manner. He began to unravel the tent from around the rest of monster's body.

"What just happened?" asked Eisley, finally finding her voice. "Did you kill that thing, Ethan?"

"I'm not sure," said Ethan.

"You unmistakably delivered the death blow," said Deerborn. "I was outside listening to the beast as it crept up near your tent. I was hoping that whatever it was would simply leave after sniffing around. But I heard someone fumbling in the tent and I knew that one of you would probably turn the lantern on. When the beast stood, I struck it from behind. I don't think my attack killed it though, Ethan." Deerborn looked at the monster again. "I believe yours did."

Deerborn was certain that this attack had been the push he needed to get the twins to see reason. It was unlikely that any of them would sleep that night, so he suggested they move from their current whereabouts. The creature was probably not alone. They packed their belongings, trying their best to salvage the tent, but it had been completely ruined by the beast. Deerborn started back towards Maridia.

"Where are you going?" asked Ethan. "That's the way we came."

Deerborn halted, closed his eyes and lowered his head as if giving up. "Surely after this you see the madness in remaining here." The Lambents stood silently. He pointed to the monster. "I have never seen a creature of this size in all of my days. Had there been more of them we would surely be dead. I'm not sure that I can protect you from what may come, as I once thought I could."

"Deerborn," said Eisley shaken but resolved. "We cannot turn back. We haven't even seen the first sign of Gloamers yet. If they are here then we need to find them so they can see the light and know that there is a place where they do not have to live in darkness."

Deerborn watched as tears filled the girl's eyes and finally he understood: they had come to *help* the Gloamers. Deerborn was moved by her compassion and submitted to their plan to head east, deeper into Gloam.

Deerborn led and the siblings followed without a word. Ethan too had been touched by his sister's fervor, and while he felt a similar need to help the Gloamers, he couldn't shake the feeling that there was something more for him in Gloam.

Chapter Fifteen

Flight

They walked as far as they possibly could, their vigilance exhausted after having no rest for nearly two days. The company had been traveling in darkness for half a week and knew not how many miles they'd traversed. Since the attack, they hadn't stopped. There was no sign of any other life and the landscape remained, as far as they could tell, unchanging.

"We have to stop. I'm so tired," said Eisley, breathless.

The others agreed and set up Deerborn's tent, their one remaining shelter. Deerborn wished aloud for a tall rock or even a hole of some sort to rest in – anything that would provide protection. Deerborn volunteered to guard over the twins while they slept, and Ethan took over once he had rested enough. The men allowed Eisley to sleep through both of their watches, an offer she was thankful for and didn't turn down.

They rested on the open plain for many hours, and had it not been for the routine appearance of the flakes, time might have ceased to exist for them. The flakes had all but dissolved when the company felt ready to proceed. Eisley, feeling as if the incident with the beast had been nothing more than a terrible nightmare, was well rested and ready to continue. Ethan, on the other hand, still yawned, but didn't complain, seeing his sister in better spirits. Deerborn showed no signs of fatigue other than the dark circles beneath his eyes.

Continuing on, the travelers began placing their markers at greater distances from one another than before to stretch out their supply.

Deerborn grew increasingly unsettled as time wore on. "If any other life exists in this desolate place, they know exactly where we are from all the screaming of that blasted creature and our lights."

It was true that the lantern's beams reflecting off the low hanging clouds would have given away their precise location. The fact that no sound had been heard since the attack concerned Deerborn. If there really were Watchers still in Gloam, they would have no trouble following their every move. His fear proved well founded. Not long after their day's journey began, footsteps rustled in the dirt not far outside the light's reach on their left side. Deerborn whispered to the twins to keep moving forward while he devised a plan of defense. Certainly it was another wolf creature, perhaps even the family of the one they'd killed.

Trekking forward they began to hear the noise from both sides and the rear. Ethan was on the verge of drawing his sword and running wildly into the darkness to face an unseen foe. As in Earnest's account, those in the darkness would not willfully enter the light surrounding the company, so Ethan felt enough protection within his glowing barrier to refrain from placing himself in unnecessary danger. Still, Earnest mentioned darts. No sooner had thoughts of projectiles entered his mind than something whistled past his head. *A dart flew into the light and directly between Deerborn and Ethan.* The latter was sure their foe wanted to take out the largest of their party first.

"Swords!" growled Deerborn, startling the twins, "Draw them!"

As the twins followed orders, the poisonous darts bombarded them from all directions. The Magic Lantern flashed a blinding light and an echoing boom released from it into the darkness. The airborne darts were diverted off course, crashing immediately to the ground. The attackers bellowed in shock and pain, momentarily forgetting their enemies. The siblings stood frozen in confusion because of what had just happened.

Deerborn turned and shouted, "The light! They won't enter it! Run toward them!"

With a fierce cry, Deerborn and the twins charged toward the veiled enemy. The sudden attack coming from the travelers caught their foes off guard. The enemy hadn't moved away from the light fast enough and their horrific forms were illuminated for the briefest of moments. The party only saw the black fur of the tall creatures, standing on hind legs. They were the same as the monster they'd encountered earlier, only now attacking with poisonous weapons. It was the Watchers.

During a moment of distraction one of the small arrows smashed the center of Deerborn's lantern and the light disappeared, leaving only Riley's lantern burning. At the same time a gap formed between the Lambents and Deerborn. The enemy used this divide to their advantage and for only a second the black devils entered the light and snatched Deerborn into the darkness.

They called out to their friend. There were too many of the Watchers for Deerborn to handle alone. Ethan moved forward, unsure of what to do next. Suddenly, they heard Deerborn's wild voice from the darkness. "Run! Run!" Then, just as quickly, his cries were silenced.

The twins followed orders. Ethan and Eisley sprinted away from Deerborn's Bane. No howls or screams of any kind came from the battle, and Ethan assumed the worst as they ran. The next few minutes were a mishmash of panicked breathing, stumbling and peering back in fear of pursers. A sharp pain formed in Ethan's side and he felt he couldn't go on much longer. Eisley was a few feet ahead, but not far enough that he could have avoided falling like he'd just seen his sister do in front of him.

The twins tumbled together down a steep hill that seemed to drop forever. When they finally came to slamming halt at the bottom, Ethan found himself hugging tightly to the lantern as the world spun around him. Eisley got to her feet, barely inside the rim of light. Ethan struggled to stand and she ran to his side. Ethan bled from his right leg and could barely get to his feet.

"Go...Go on!" cried Ethan breathlessly. "Take the lantern and go!"

"No," shouted Eisley. "I wont leave you!"

"You have to!" yelled Ethan. His breathing eased and the pain in his leg mellowed into an even throb.

"I'd rather be eaten by those…those things!"

They stared at each other stubbornly. The darkness around them was also silent.

"Where did they go?" whispered Ethan.

"I don't think they're following us," said Eisley. Then the magnitude of what had just transpired overtook her. "Oh, Deerborn…oh no! Poor Abril. It's all our fault."

Eisley seemed frantic. Ethan grabbed her shoulders and looked her square in the eyes. "There's nothing we can do about Deerborn right now. We have to keep moving. Just because they're not following us doesn't mean they're not coming back for us." He looked around, as if expecting a Watcher to appear at any moment. "They could be here with us right now, listening."

Eisley regained her composure.

"I have to keep you safe," continued Ethan, holding Eisley close. "Do you hear me? I have to!"

Eisley nodded.

"Did you see how the lantern protected us when those darts came at us?" asked Ethan.

Again Eisley nodded.

"It *does* have some sort of power and now the Watchers know that as well. That might work to our advantage."

Eisley listened intently, allowing what had happened with the lantern to sink in.

"We have to stay inside the light and we have to keep moving," continued Ethan.

"Can you do that?" asked Eisley looking at Ethan's injured leg.

"I think so." Ethan tested his ability to walk.

"Good," said Eisley. "Because I'm not leaving you here alone."

They headed off as fast as they could manage in some unknown direction. As they walked, both thought of Deerborn. They had seen him pulled from the light like a grape from the vine. Now they were totally alone. Or so they hoped.

Chapter Sixteen
To Speak of Seeing

Traveling injured was harder than Ethan had expected. His pain grew until it was all he could think of. The frazzled Lambents stopped continually in what seemed like endless hours of travel so that Ethan could nurse his leg. Finally, the aching became more than he could bear to travel on and so the siblings paused for a more extended break in the eternal night.

The twins lay on the hard dusty surface of Gloam saying very little as they peered into the emptiness. The darkness seemed to press against the lantern light trying desperately to swallow it whole. Or maybe this was a figment of their imagination, intensified by the loss of Deerborn. He had been the reason Ethan and Eisley were not overwhelmed by the bleak darkness. His presence brought security, now stolen. It felt as if despair was creeping in with each breath. Would they ever be free from its hold? Poor Deerborn. It was their fault that Abril would now spend the rest of her days alone, waiting for word of what had become of her beloved husband. Nearly all was despair now. Only one sliver of comfort remained – the Magic Lantern. The Lambent heirloom shone brightly around the twins, despite the threatening darkness. Somehow the light emanated an odd solace with each pulsating beam. It brought both comforting memories and a longing for home. These peaceful meditations were soon squelched by the competing gloom bringing ideas of their beacon of hope drawing more curious eyes toward them. Luminosity fighting for a stronger foot hold – it had been the lantern that saved them. Then despair, rising again – surely their absence had caused only hopelessness…distress…even anguish. Where were these horrible thoughts coming from?

"I wonder how long Mother and Father searched for us?" asked Ethan.

"Searched?" asked Eisley. "Do you really think they've given up looking for us?"

"It has been well over a fortnight since we saw them last," said Ethan. "How long do you think they would search?"

"As long as it took to find us, I'd imagine," answered Eisley, hopefully.

"Do you think they would come here?" asked Ethan.

"Yes," said Eisley. "If they actually thought *we'd* come to Gloam, *they'd* come."

Grandpa Emmett shared their adventurous spirit and knew they'd travel to Gloam. Now, for the first time, Ethan felt a pang of regret, not only for dragging his sister and Deerborn into this forsaken place, but possibly even his family too. If Grandpa or Father had picked up on his and his sister's trail, would they find Maridia and learn of the siblings' recent visit? Would they discover their path toward Gloam? Would they brave danger's path to save he and Eisley, forfeiting their own lives in the process? The Watchers were a formidable foe, even managing to take down the Captain of the Maridian Guard. The only sure protection had proven to be the Lantern and the twins had it, not his family. Ethan couldn't bear the thought any longer. Despair. Now all he could hope for was that his parents had stayed in Luminae to await their return. They wouldn't return though. Only despair.

Trying to fight off the building sadness, Ethan thought of other matters that only led deeper into worry. Thinking of eventual sleep led to the need for cover, which led to their lack of shelter. They had lost their tent in the first bout with the lone Watcher. Deerborn had carried the other tent and who knew what had become of his belongings? He had carried the bulk of their rations as well. Would they starve now? What about water? They were nearly out. Such despair. It was in this state of helplessness that the twins both began to nod off to sleep.

Some time later Ethan and Eisley awoke to the long forgotten feeling of rain. This was the first time it had rained since their journey began. They knew not how long they'd been asleep but the light rainfall seemed to startle them in to a new-found state of alertness. Eisley immediately stood, shaking off sleep. She listened intently – there was no other sound save the pitter-patter of the rain hitting the dry ground. A light breeze began wafting the, ever so slight, smell of salt their way. It smelled like the ocean. Were they in some kind of coastal area?

"Should we move on?" asked Eisley, feeling energized and alert.

She turned to find Ethan having a difficult time getting to his feet.

"You look bad," said Eisley.

"Yeah," said Ethan. "I think the rest really stiffened my leg."

"Can you keep going?" Eisley questioned as she knelt to give her brother aid.

"I might be able to go a little further but – wait – what is that? GET BEHIND ME!" Ethan suddenly screamed. Something moved quietly into the light behind his sister. Eisley spun around. Together the twins looked on in horror as a tall, furry, wolf-like creature crept into the edge of the light. The monster was walking on its hind legs. Knowing that Ethan couldn't run, Eisley drew her sword. Ethan did the same.

Strangely, the Watcher did not advance. They waited for an attack but none came. Then a most unexpected thing happened. The creature lifted its hands to its head, and the Lambents raised their swords a little higher. The monster clawed at its mouth and then suddenly the head of the thing dropped backwards off its shoulders, revealing a person. There before them stood a man, if you could truly call him a man. He didn't look much older than the twins.

What followed was the most curious of all. For a time the newcomer seemed to forget that Ethan and Eisley were staring at him with swords held at the ready. The man seemed to be completely mystified by the light, or rather by the fact that he could see himself. The twins were given a start as the man wrestled away from the rest of the fur he wore. The Watchers weren't animals at all. But wait – perhaps this wasn't a

Watcher. This fellow could have killed a Watcher and now wears his skin like a coat.

After the visitor stepped from his furry overalls he began to examine himself, revealing to the twins a ghost white man wearing nothing more than a loincloth. The specter-like figure stood silently in the rain, staring at his body as if seeing it for the first time. And maybe he was. Ethan and his sister carried the only source of light in all of Gloam.

The man started by examining his hands, holding them up to his face and bending his fingers in and out. Then his eyes receded down his arms to where they met his torso. He continued in this manner until he looked over the whole of his body ending with his legs and feet and then bending to touch his toes. It was like watching a baby who had noticed its legs for the first time. Then the man looked towards Ethan and Eisley and took in their appearance. Ethan felt he saw, distinctly, in the man's eyes the very moment that the visitor had realized that both he and the ones standing before him were of the same race. A look of astonishment came over the stranger's face as he spoke his first words, which gave the twins a jump.

"Hullo," said he.

"Hello," said Ethan and Eisley reluctantly.

"I am called Canis," said the man.

Ethan pointed at himself, giving his name and then pointed at Eisley, giving hers.

"Hullo, Ethan and Eisley," said Canis.

The strange character stood silent. It was apparent that he was still getting used to seeing. He had a look of pain upon his face. Ethan decided that if he himself had discovered a new sense, previously unknown to him, he'd probably don the same expression as the Gloamer.

"Where do you come from?" This time when the stranger spoke, the twins noticed a slight trill in his voice – an almost singsong quality.

"We come from Glæm," answered Ethan.

"Glæm," said Canis as if testing the sound of a new word with his tongue. "And is this Glæm, as you call it, beyond the Breath-of-Smarr?"

"The what?" asked Ethan.

"The Breath-of-Smarr," restated the stranger. "Do you not know of the great wind that blows ever outward on the edge of Gloam?"

Ethan recalled the fierce gale that nearly drove them backwards at the Deadwood and the entrance to Gloam. "Oh, yes, our land is beyond that."

What a curious name for the wind.

"Is the wind actually the Breath-of-Smarr?" asked Eisley.

"Humph," said Canis with something resembling a giggle and an amused look on his face. "No. Smarr is a myth. The Breath-of-Smarr is nothing more than wind," though it took him a minute to actually formulate this answer. "Are you familiar with the word *myth*?"

"Yes," answered Ethan. "But do you mean to say that Smarr isn't actually here in Gloam?"

"No, he is not," answered Canis. "There are those of us who believe that he might have existed at one time, though very few of our kind actually believe he still does. Evidence does not exist of such a one as Smarr."

"Isn't the darkness evidence enough?" asked Eisley.

The newcomer seemed confused by this statement. "What is this 'darkness' that you speak of?"

"The darkness is all of the blackness that surrounds your land," said Ethan. "It's the inability to see."

"And what does 'see' mean? Is that what you call being able to realize from here?" The curious man pointed to his eyes.

"Yes," replied Ethan. He had never thought of seeing as realizing.

"It is true that we in Gloam have never been able to do this 'see'," answered Canis thoughtfully. "Does it happen often in your land, this Glæm, as you call it?"

"As long as our eyes are open," said Eisley, pointing to her own eyes, with a smile. "We live in a land with light."

"Light," said Canis, "I have heard this word 'light' before. We have a song that tells of it in our land's past."

Ethan carefully adjusted his stance.

Canis noticed. "Are you injured?"

Ethan was reluctant to share this information to a stranger and did not answer for a moment.

"I mean you no harm. Please sit so that you may alleviate some of your pain," said the Gloamer, understanding Ethan's silence.

"Are you a Watcher?" asked Eisley directly.

"I am very sorry but I'm afraid that I'm not familiar with this word 'watcher' either," said Canis.

Ethan reluctantly sat down while addressing his sister. "Remember, Earnest gave the Watchers that name."

"Oh, that's right," replied Eisley. "I'd forgotten."

"We have been attacked," Ethan said to Canis, "by a group of five or six creatures. They...they took a friend of ours. My sister and I were able to get away but I hurt my leg in the flight."

"Did they use any weapons against you?" asked Canis, seeming more concerned now.

"Yes," answered Ethan. "Some sort of projectile or dart."

With this news Canis peered, overly dramatically, across the landscape.

Bending to the ground Canis picked up the furry thing he'd been wearing. He held it out and asked, "Was its form similar to this?"

"Exactly like that," answered Eisley.

"You speak of the Squalor," said Canis a hint of fear in his voice. He sounded almost as if he'd taken on a few minor notes in his speech now. "They are the creatures who rule over Gloam. You're sure this is what attacked you?"

Ethan and Eisley gave an affirmative nod to which Canis did not respond. He had never *seen* someone answer a question. Realizing their error, Ethan *said* that they were positive.

"Was your encounter with the Squalor far from here?" questioned Canis.

"We have come a good distance, I think," said Ethan. "My leg has kept us from going very far though."

"Was it above the Down that you crossed paths with them?" asked Canis.

"If you mean the enormous slope away behind us then yes, it was above that," guessed Ethan.

"Good," said Canis, chancing a step closer towards the twins, "It is very rare that the Squalor venture into the Down." Then coming closer still, Canis reiterated that he meant the twins no harm and asked Ethan if he could examine his injured leg. Ethan agreed, apprehensively because Canis had refitted himself in the nightmarish coat he'd been wearing. The Gloamer cautiously knelt to inspect the wound. To Ethan's amazement, the man closed his eyes to do so. Canis felt Ethan's leg with a very careful procedure that was apparently acquired by not having sight.

Once he'd finished he opened his eyes and said, "Your leg is not broken, though it can still be harmful to you. You need to have it treated soon."

"How?" answered Ethan, not sure that he really wanted to hear the answer.

"There is a settlement not too far from here called By Down," answered Canis. "If you would allow me, I could carry you there and have the village's restorer administer a treatment for your wound."

Ethan didn't see any other option. Eisley also agreed to going. By no means had Canis gained the twins' confidence, but whether he was friend or foe mattered little at this point. Ethan could either accept Canis' help or he and Eisley would have to wait for some less helpful company to arrive. Ethan sheathed his sword and accepted the offer. Eisley put away her blade as well.

Canis was much stronger than the siblings had guessed. He tossed Ethan upon his back easily. Ethan's face became buried in the matted, smelly, wet fur of the Squalor covering. His stomach gave a sickening turn as a question came to his mind. "How is it," began Ethan, "that you came by the Squalor fur you're wearing?"

"The Squalor are not a very affectionate race," answered Canis. "They leave their own for dead without any thought of remorse. I came across this one months ago not far from here. It had apparently wandered into the Downs to die. I was cold and needed a coat," he answered simply.

Chapter Seventeen
By Down

The journey to By Down took several hours despite the speed at which the Gloamer moved. Canis ran nearly the entire way with Ethan on his back, stopping only twice for water and rest. Ethan hadn't been the least hindrance to the dark dweller. Eisley enjoyed the traveling because it had given her a chance to spread her wings, in a manner of speaking, and do some much-needed running. She had to admit that there was something peculiar about Canis' strength. It didn't seem natural for anyone to be able to carry another over such a great distance at such a great speed. But, then, nothing about Gloam was natural. Even with her suspicions of Canis, she remained thankful for his help.

Without the sun, the twins were completely oblivious to the time of day. There had been flakes to give some indication of the time; however, since entering the Down, many hours had passed without their appearance. They should have seen them by now. Ethan thought not having some measure of time might eventually lead to hysteria. He hadn't realized how much he relied on time until he lost track of it. It wasn't long before his fear was relieved. Outside of the Down, after they reascended the massive slope, much further north of where they'd taken their fall, the curious ground covering reappeared.

When Canis noticed the flakes a bizarre thing happened: he retrieved a sampling from the ground and began to eat it. The twins had not thought the flakes edible, much less the main source of the Gloamer's diet, as they soon discovered. Famished, the Lambents decided to partake with Canis. The flakes had a pleasant taste, much like a mixture of bread and potatoes. Because the flakes were so delicate and crunchy they tasted very similar to a thinly sliced, fried potato. At any rate, they were nourishing and welcomed.

"How does this stuff grow?" asked Eisley.

"The nån?" asked Canis holding up a flake.

"Yes," answered Eisley. "The nån, did you say?"

"Yes, nån," said Canis. "It has always appeared with our waking from sleep. "Does not Glæm have nån?"

"No." said the twins.

"Then what do you eat?" questioned the Gloamer.

"We eat meat and vegetables," answered Ethan.

"And fruit," added Eisley.

"What are these, vegetables, as you call them?" asked Canis.

"Vegetables are similar to nån, I suppose," said Ethan, "because they come from the ground. But how does nån grow? Do you plant it?"

"Plant?" asked Canis.

"Yes," answered Ethan. "We have to plant, or bury, a tiny thing called a seed in the soil and then with the help of the sun, water and time the seed grows into something we can eat." Then he considered something: "But of course you wouldn't know what the sun is either would you?" Ethan peered toward the impenetrable clouds above that were certainly there, though he couldn't see them.

"No, I'm afraid I do not know of the sun," said Canis.

"The sun," said Eisley, "is much like this lantern here. Both give off light but the sun is a bigger light that shines down from the heavens."

"There are so many strange things you make me aware of," chimed Canis with a hint of longing in his musical tone. "I know nothing of these 'heavens' you speak of either, but I *have* heard the word 'lantern.'"

"You have?" said Ethan.

"Yes. The *lantern* and the *light* are in the same song of our past. Would you like to hear it?"

The twins wanted eagerly to hear the song. Canis began to sing. Though the song, as Canis sang it, was unworldlier than anything the twins had ever heard. Words cannot describe the sounds and notes that came forth from the Gloamer. The song went as follows:

From a land to us unknown,
Came forth something that shone,
Into the land of Gloam,
Carried by a strangely one,
The Magic Lantern divided up our homes,
Bringing forth a terrible light,
That came to terrify the souls of Gloam,
The light did wrench and tear,

From us those we hold dear,
Never again to be known

Canis opened his eyes and there sat the silent listeners. Canis looked as if the verses had awakened an understanding within him. "There are many words that I have never understood in this song until now – the light...the lantern. Is this the same lantern that the song speaks of?"

"Yes," murmured Ethan. Canis seemed remarkably calm for having just recounted the terror the lantern had inflicted upon Gloam. Ethan looked away from Canis feeling ashamed for some reason. Ethan couldn't form words to speak.

"I'm sorry but your song isn't correct," admitted Eisley.

"Why do you say this?" asked Canis. The Gloamer remained motionless except for the slightest movement in his eyes as they came to rest upon Eisley. His mood was simply unreadable, even eerie.

"The lantern wasn't brought here to terrify the Gloamers. The Gloamers that left your land with Riley did so because they wanted to."

"Riley?"

"That was name of the stranger that you sang about."

"How do you know this?"

"All of Glæm knows of the Boy of Legend and his story. We celebrate his heroic journey into Gloam."

"Boy of Legend...Heroic?"

"Yes, he is a hero and we are related to him."

Ethan couldn't believe that Eisley was being so forthwith about everything. From Canis' point of view the lantern showing up had been a horrible moment in Gloam's past.

"Do your people really believe that Riley took Gloamers captive?" asked Ethan, finally speaking.

"Yes, we do," said Canis, shifting his eyes toward Ethan.

"But it's a lie," protested Eisley.

"Please, please friends," said Canis, standing to his feet. "I can obviously see that the light means us no harm. I just need time to think on what this may mean about our histories."

"Hang on, do you make songs of your histories? Is that how you keep track of what's happened?" gawked Ethan. It made perfect sense. That would be why Jukes and Miss Naava said they had never seen a book from Gloam.

"Of course, we remember our past through song. Generation to generation. Do you not?"

"No," laughed Ethan. "We document our histories in things called books."

"Books? How?"

"By placing markings that we understand on an empty surface."

"So you aren't taught to remember everything?"

"Of course not," giggled Eisley.

What Canis was suggesting seemed impossible to actually do. The Gloamers were apparently much more intelligent than any outsider supposed.

"It sounds as if these books are doing all the work for your minds," declared Canis with a harmonious laugh.

"Yes," agreed Ethan, "I guess they are."

Feeling nourished from the nån, the travelers left their resting spot and began the final leg of their journey to By Down. When they drew close to the settlement, the twins began to hear a horrible howling noise that rose and fell – the sounds of surprise and panic in the darkness close by.

"I should have told you to remove the light," said Canis. "The people on the edge of town have 'seen,' as you call it, for the first time. They are reacting as I thought they might."

"Should I turn off the lantern?" asked Ethan.

"It is too late for that I fear," said Canis. "I must go before them and try to explain the situation. Remain here until I return."

"Will they try to attack us?" said Eisley.

"No. I believe they're too frightened for that," answered Canis.

Eisley moved closer to her brother's side.

"What will you tell them?" asked Ethan, putting his arm around his sister.

"The truth, of course," answered Canis.

It took longer for Canis to return than expected. When he did come back, he explained that he had a difficult time trying to convince the By Downers that the light was not harmful. As with Canis, those in the town had been utterly shocked by their newly discovered sense. The groans and cries had indeed been induced by this new sensory awakening. What had taken Canis the most time, however, was waiting for the Gloamers to decide which one of their people would act as the ambassador to the alien party. It was decided that the Restorer would be the one to enter the light for the sake of aiding Ethan.

The Restorer spent a fair amount of time inspecting his own form upon entering the light. The Elderly man had long snow-white hair that seemed to disappear at his shoulders. This was only an optical illusion or a camouflaging effect for the man's hair was much longer than shoulder length but his skin was so white that his hair simply blended in where it lay upon his body. He wondered if all Gloamers had long unkempt hair. This was probably the case; what purpose would visual conceit have in a world without sight? Looking at the man, standing there half naked reminded Ethan of the temperature – oddly enough it was very pleasant. So much had been happening that he hadn't taken into account the fact that it was no longer freezing. This frustrated Ethan to no end because it defied everything he knew of the physical world.

Once the man satisfied his own curiosities he came to inspect Ethan's injury. Upon closer inspection the man wore a fur of some sort around his mid-section, very unlike the Squalor's fur that Canis wore. Ethan made a mental note to inquire of the existing animal life of Gloam at a later time. For now, his mind was on the ghost of a man who performed the same scanning technique that Canis had done on his leg.

Thus far the man hadn't spoken a single word to Ethan or his sister. Bothered by this, Ethan said hello, waiting of a reply.

There was no reply.

"Thank you for your help, sir," said Ethan.

The man still said nothing. It was possible the man was deaf. Ethan shuddered at the thought of being without sight and hearing in this land. The Restorer's eyes seemed to answer one question, for in them was a look of having discovered the source of his patient's pain. The man stood and walked to the edge of the light to meet Canis. The man then *whispered* something to Canis and disappeared.

"Wait a minute," said Ethan. "Why would he not talk to me?"

Canis pondered over this question for an unnatural amount of time before stuttering, "Uh...they are more frightened than you know."

"Of what?" mused Eisley. "We are hardly a threat. Especially with Ethan hurt as he is."

"I am aware of that," replied Canis sounding a bit on edge. "However, it isn't you that they are afraid of."

"The light then?" asked Eisley.

Canis did not answer. Instead, he turned to greet an approaching figure. The Restorer returned carrying a flat rock with a muddy paste plastered upon its surface. The old man bent down and began to apply the paste to Ethan's leg. This reminded him very much of the Healer's concoction back in Maridia, although the affect was much different. At first Ethan felt a cold, tingling sensation, followed by a warm feeling that grew to an unbearable temperature. Ethan collapsed and knew no more.

Chapter Eighteen
Dispelled

Ethan awoke what seemed to be moments later. He couldn't remember, but thought he might have been poisoned. Unable to focus his eyes properly, he lay there listening to the sounds around him. From somewhere not too far away, he heard an ensemble of voices sounding as if they were singing separate songs at the same time.

Ethan squinted, straining to see, and found that he was alone in the luminescence of the lantern. From the voices he knew that a group of Gloamers must be gathered just beyond the reach of the light. In the midst of the chorus, one sweet voice that was less musical but much warmer began to stand out. The voice reminded him of home – it was his sister speaking.

"Eisley?"

Ethan sat up. His joints were very stiff.

"I'm here," came a voice from the darkness.

A moment later Eisley was there at her brother's side.

"Are you okay? How do you feel? I've been so worried about you."

"I'm alright, I think."

Very slowly he got to his feet and tested his ability to walk.

"Yes, my leg feels much better. How long have I been out?"

"You've been asleep for days."

Ethan was confounded. It felt as if the Restorer had treated him only moments ago.

Eisley handed a container of water to Ethan. He drank deeply, his parched throat refreshed by the liquid.

"What happened to me?" he asked.

"The same thing that happens to anyone who receives the medicine that you were given, according to Canis. He said the paste the Restorer put on your leg caused you to go into a deep sleep. Apparently it is a very fortunate side affect of the medicine. Without it, the pain of the healing process would be to hard to take."

"Where is Canis now?" questioned Ethan.

"Canis is in By Down because the Elders have summoned him there."

"What were you doing in the dark?"

"I was talking with my company!"

Excitedly, Eisley beckoned Ethan to follow her out of the light. Ethan followed reluctantly. She led him a few paces into the deep darkness and stopped. Here, the choral voices could be heard distinctly. They sounded beautiful.

"Who are they?" asked Ethan.

"They're Gloamers from By Down!"

She introduced her brother.

"Hullo," came a chorus from the darkness.

"Hello," chuckled Ethan. "There are so many," he whispered to Eisley.

She too gave a little laugh and said, "Yes, well they didn't all come at once. Nellek and Eecyak came first and then the next day they brought the others."

"Are they not afraid?" asked Ethan.

"More curious than afraid, I think," said Eisley.

"We came to learn about you and about your Magic Lantern," sang Eecyak.

"I've been telling them stories of our home for quite some time. They find Glæm fascinating, though I don't think they believe all that I'm saying," said Eisley.

"Would it not be easier for us to go into the town instead of having all the By Downers come out here?" asked Ethan. "We could take the lantern into town..."

"That would not be permissible," interrupted Canis, suddenly standing behind the twins. Neither heard his approach. "It is the wish of the Elders of By Down that we bring the lantern no closer than we already have."

Ethan heard the other Gloamers whispering among themselves after Canis spoke, though he couldn't make out what they were saying.

"Canis tried to convince the Elders that the light is harmless," said Eisley. "But they still won't let us near the town."

"Have any of these Gloamers gone into the light yet?" asked Ethan.

"No," answered Eisley. "They're still too afraid."

"None of it matters now," said Canis. "We have been told to leave."

"What! Why?" exclaimed Eisley.

"The Elders believe that we have brought misfortune upon By Down. They are not at all pleased the By Downers are beginning to congregate so close to the light, or that they are so eager to converse with you, Eisley."

"Can't their minds be changed?" asked Ethan.

"I'm afraid not," answered Canis. "The elder's vote was unanimous."

"When must we leave?" Eisley's voice sounded quietly in the dark.

"They have been gracious enough to allow us to remain here until we have slept, but then we must go," said Canis.

Pleading, Eisley said, "Can't I go to the Elders and try to change their minds?"

"That would not be a wise decision. Remember, they have requested that neither of you nor your lantern come any closer."

"Our curiosity has caused your banishment from here. We greatly apologize."

"No, please don't apologize Nellek," said Eisley. "There is nothing to be sorry for. Meeting all of you is the very reason that Ethan and I have traveled so far. You have come to learn more about us and so I intend to tell you as much as I can."

"That would not be prudent," said Canis. "Their continued presence here is causing much tension."

"If they don't want me to have these conversations with my company, then I suggest they come and tell me so. Otherwise, I intend to finish my stories."

Ethan imagined the stubborn glint in his sister's eyes as she defied Canis' advice. He was surprised by her resolve.

"Very well," replied Canis, shortly. The twins heard him walk away.

Eisley sat down and continued the story she'd been telling the Gloamers before they had been interrupted. Ethan decided to sit next to her and join the conversation. He listened to her as she told of something that seemed so trivial to him. She recounted a trip their family had taken to Eleora, a small town in the northernmost parts of Glæm. The trip took place some years back and had been rather uneventful. Northern Glæm was one of the quietest and most restful places to visit in all of their homeland, which is why the Lambent family had gone there. But Eisley hadn't been telling this story to describe their destination, but to express the beauty of the landscape they traveled over on the way there. She told of the lush green Plains of Eron, the wide, blue Yitta River, and of the snow-capped and unreachable Temiran Mountains to the north. She described the enormous waves that crashed upon the western shores of Glæm. In truth, she was merely painting a picture of what it was like to *see* things, hoping it would spur a desire within her audience to go to such a place. Even though the Gloamers had no idea what colors were or what it would look like to see water crash into something, they were captivated by the telling of the story. The next few hours were filled with laughter, which Ethan and Eisley needed desperately, more than either yet knew.

Chapter Nineteen
The Adventure Song

The time for sleep came and went and the twins prepared, once again, to set off into the darkness. They packed their things and strapped on their swords and carryalls. To make their trip easier, the twins decided not to bring along their armor. It was simply too much to heave over great distances any longer. A few of the By Downers came to say their goodbyes. They brought with them animal skins filled with water. These were given to the three travelers as parting gifts to replace the smaller flasks that had been Deerborn's. While the skins were a little heavier than the old ones, the twins were grateful for the supply. Before leaving, the travelers ate their fill of nån.

Ethan did his best to mask the apprehension of the coming journey. Canis suggested they travel north toward The Rise, Canis' home, which he explained was a settlement similar to By Down. Canis reasoned that they might have better luck in a place where the people knew him. Having no better ideas and no option but to trust their guide, the Lambents agreed to his proposition. Ethan and Eisley feared moving deeper into Gloam, risking the chance of encountering the Squalor again. This prospect didn't seem to affect Canis in the least, though he'd seemed fearful of them when the twins first met him.

It seemed their path was set. Eisley hadn't wanted to get her new friends in trouble with the Elders of the town, so she didn't put up a fuss about moving on even though she wanted to stay to tell them more about the Light of Glæm. Ethan had not been given the time that his sister had to develop a relationship with the Gloamers. What regret he did feel was more for Eisley's sake. He saw how much she had grown to care for those living in the darkness. So it was with these thoughts that they began their march into the unknown.

They traveled for hours in silence, finally broken by a nagging question on the tip of Ethan's tongue: "Canis, if you live in the north, what were you doing so far south in the Down?"

"I wondered when that would come up. I am what is called a Gatherer."

"What's that?" asked Eisley.

"Do you remember when I first met you and I told you that the Squalor leave their own to die?"

The twins nodded, a gesture that Canis was becoming more familiar with.

"Well, a Gatherer is one who combs the land in search of the dead Squalor. We take the hides and sell them in the towns."

"But then why were you so far from home? Are there no Squalor in the north?" asked Ethan.

"That is correct," answered Canis. "The Squalor inhabit only the southern lands."

Canis would say no more of his trade. In fact not long after this exchange, Canis decided he'd had quite enough of trying to navigate with his eyes and decided to walk ahead of the twins outside the light. This act began to separate the Lambents from their guide. It seemed Canis no longer had any desire to be with them. Because of the growing tension, the thought crossed Ethan's mind to turn back and attempt to find their way out of Gloam. He didn't know whether his sister would agree to this or not, but finally, during a short break, when Canis reentered the light to rest with the twins, Ethan asked Eisley about the prospect of turning back. Eisley was still set on continuing their journey. Ethan hadn't noticed until now but sometime during the last week, the mysterious draw to Gloam had faded in him. He didn't know why, when Eisley appeared to still have that feeling inside her. While they talked, Canis listened to their conversation but never joined in.

Ethan did not like the escalating sense of being trapped in Gloam. His feeling of despair started to intensify as the relationship between the twins and Canis worsened. The Gloamer was always just beyond the light, only coming back to join them for rest and sleep. Canis even began to venture off during their times of rest, saying he'd heard something or wanting to scout ahead to make sure they wouldn't surprise anyone with the lantern again.

Ethan began to think that Gloam hadn't many inhabitants at all. They had only come upon one single village in all their time there. He looked to the lantern on several occasions and wondered if its light would ever give up, leaving them at the mercy of the darkness. As they traveled, Ethan and Eisley watched the darkness gain ground on the light. The forces seemed to fight against each other. The darkness closed in on them one minute, and the next, the light pushed out against the darkness again. But the lantern's light shone strong. The travelers remained silent most of the time. Ethan and Eisley's hopes of grand adventure and bringing salvation to Gloam had all but vanished; it dissolved a little more with each step they took, and Ethan felt as if the hope was literally being drained from him. He never spoke of this with Eisley who, unknown to him, felt the same way.

One particular day when Eisley felt that joy was nearly gone, she started singing a song her father had written about the Boy of Legend. The Adventure Song, as it was called, was written to commemorate Riley's journey. Every year at the celebration of the Awakening, the Lambent family gathered around the fireplace and sang this song. When he heard Eisley singing, Ethan joined his sister.

My heart is racing
at the thought of what's ahead,
And what adventures will unfold,
The story of our lives awaits around the bend,
How will our journey hence be told?

Though the way may seem unclear,
We'll carry on to lands unknown,

Though the night seems much to fear,
Heart hold fast to where you're drawn.

Traveling on the heels of one who's come before,
His standard we will gladly bear,
We'll cross the mountains
and the forests to beyond,
Into the darkness if we dare.

Though the way may seem unclear,
We'll carry on to lands unknown,
Though the night seems much to fear,
Heart hold fast to where you're drawn.

Ethan considered the last line of the song, remembering the distinct feeling of being drawn towards Gloam so many weeks ago. He wondered now if the darkness had indeed taken it from him.

It was extraordinary to hear the song ring out across the vast night. A noticeable change took place in Canis and he walked with the twins once again. Though it started small, this led eventually to conversation like they had had many days before. All three travelers were cheered, and a change came over the Gloamer's entire countenance.

Ethan and Eisley both sensed a longing in Canis' continuous questions about Glæm. This notion was discussed between the twins on one of Canis' scouting leaves. His absences happened less and less with each passing day. The twins had not expected the journey to The Rise to take so long. Surprisingly enough, even with the great distances, it wasn't a physically hard journey. The travelers stopped multiple times a day and often found small streams that had kept their water supply full. The nån continued to appear every morning keeping their hunger satisfied, and Ethan's injured leg felt better than ever before.

The long journey gave Ethan ample time to process everything that had happened since leaving By Down. One thing that had most definitely not happened was an encounter with Smarr, which according to Canis, didn't even exist.

When Ethan brought the subject up again Canis said, "It seems to certainly be a fairy-tale given the lack of evidence."

But was there really a lack of evidence? Was not the darkness itself proof enough of some power? Just as the light was evidence of another sort of power? Ethan recalled his talks with Jukes about the Creator. The greatest evidence of the Light being the Maker of all things was the simple fact that the light existed and warmed the lives of those who lived in it. There was evidence in a changed heart, as well. Or at least that is what Ethan had been told his whole life.

Still, Ethan was certain that he'd yet to experience the Light changing him. Jukes had seen the evidence of a Creator yet still denied it. The Overseer's question came screaming back into Ethan's mind – if the light truly created everything, then why does the darkness exist as well? Ethan had no answer. Why *would* the Light allow the oppressive darkness to infect the world? That is, if the Light is truly the Creator, and if there is even a Creator at all. This was the one and only barrier to Ethan truly grasping his family's beliefs in a tangible way. He wasn't sure if he'd ever get around this problem.

Chapter Twenty
A Breach of Trust

Ethan, Eisley and Canis had been traveling in a northerly direction for weeks when they abruptly changed course and began to go west.

"Why are we changing direction all of a sudden?" asked Ethan, after Canis turned hurriedly from the trail they were on.

"There is a danger," answered Canis. "Come, we must travel faster."

The twins struggled to keep up with the frantic pace of their guide. They were puzzled, for they had not seen or heard anything out of the ordinary in the dark, silent country.

"What danger?" asked Eisley. She looked from side to side, expecting something in the dark to dart into the light.

"I will explain later. For now you must trust me. We need to move quickly."

The empty plains eventually gave way to rocky crags, and as the travelers maneuvered through them, Ethan's curiosity got the best of him and he felt he couldn't go on without knowing what peril they were presently trying to elude.

"Please tell us what we are running from," said Ethan.

Canis looked away from Ethan and with a deep, woeful sigh he said, "I will tell you but first we must find a more suitable place to talk."

Canis led the way between high rocks that surrounded them from all sides, save the narrow opening where they had entered. Feeling satisfied that they were safe, Canis began, "I am not who you think I am. I am not a Gatherer. In fact, there is no such thing," he admitted regretfully.

"No such thing?" questioned Eisley, with a touch of fear in her voice. "Then what are you?"

"I am a Hand of Smarr."

"What?" cried Ethan. "Smarr? I thought you said he wasn't real?"

"That too was a lie," admitted Canis. "I am afraid that Smarr is very real."

"And you work for him?" asked Eisley, on the verge of tears. "You are a Watcher!"

"I am."

Ethan drew his sword feeling more full of rage than ever before. The Gloamer was strong, but he wouldn't go down without a fight.

"Please, I am not going to harm you," said the traitor. "But there is more that you must hear while there is still time."

"Lies!" shouted Ethan. "Do you expect us to believe anything you tell us at this point!"

Eisley laid her hand upon Ethan's out-stretched arm and he lowered the sword a little.

"Let him speak," she said.

Canis was taken aback by Eisley's calm.

"Eisley, you can't possibly want to hear what he has to say!" protested Ethan. "He has been leading us into a trap! We can't believe him now!"

"I'm afraid you have no choice at the moment," said Canis. "You are right, Ethan. I have been leading you into a trap since the moment we met. Nay, even before."

"Before we met?" asked Eisley.

"I was there when your friend was taken."

"Deerborn?" Eisley began to lose her composure. "He is dead because of you?!" she shouted. Her curtain of calm came crashing down as she ran at Canis.

"Please, Eisley, listen to me." Canis effortlessly blocked the blows she threw at him. "Deerborn is alive!"

"What?!" She suddenly relented in her attack.

"He is alive," repeated Canis. "He is being held at The Rise."

"In your town?" said Ethan.

"It is not a town. The Rise is the mountain upon which Smarr lives. I was taking you directly to him."

"Can we save Deerborn?" questioned Eisley, ignoring the further betrayal. "Can we get to him?"

"That I do not know," said Canis. "For I know nothing of Smarr's dwelling place."

"How is that possible? You're his servant?" said Ethan.

"Though we are called the Hands of Smarr, we have never had physical contact with him. He speaks to our minds. That is how he first drew me unto himself. I have been in his service ever since."

"Why are you telling us these things now?" asked Ethan. "Why not just finish what you started."

"Because I have come to understand that Smarr is the malicious one and not you or the light you carry; we have been led to believe otherwise. We have been deceived. I have pleaded with the other Hands of Smarr to let you go. They will not and they know of my disloyalty to them. They are tracking us even now."

"So when you left us all those times...you were reporting back to the other Watchers?" asked Ethan.

"Precisely," answered Canis, suddenly cocking his head to the side, like a dog would, to listen. He heard something in the darkness. "There is more that I must confess. You were not banished from By Down. That was my doing."

"Then why did you allow me to speak with the By Downers at all?" asked Eisley.

"Because I found no harm in what you were telling them. In fact, I too was curious about the things you were saying," answered Canis. "Torolf, my leader was afraid that your conversations would find their way back to Smarr, so he ordered me to leave town with you continue to The Rise. He told me to make up a reason for our abrupt departure and..."

Canis, stopped short and began to listen more intently.

"What is it?" asked Ethan. "Are the other Watchers near?"

"We need to leave this place, we're cornered here." said Eisley, looking at their surroundings.

"It's to late," said Canis. "They're already here!"

Four horrific wolf-like figures could now be seen on the rocks above. They came moving into the edges of the light from all directions. The Lambents were surrounded.

One of the Watchers dropped off the rocks, landing in a crouch near Canis.

"Canis," greeted the dark figure as he pulled the fur back from his head, revealing a man's blindfolded face.

"Torolf," said Canis, moving into a defensive stance.

"Traitor!" shouted the other. "You have spoken too many secrets here. You will speak no more."

"Why do you cover your eyes Torolf?" mocked Canis. "Are you afraid of the light?"

"Only afraid of it poisoning my mind, as it has yours! Hands of Smarr, take them!"

The other Watchers leaped from the rocks to surround Canis and the twins. The Lambents drew their twin swords. Canis leapt headlong into Torolf with a snarl. The twins positioned themselves back to back to better protect each other, a tactic they'd learned from Deerborn. Ethan and Eisley were outnumbered as three Watchers pressed in on them. The enemies crawled towards the siblings on all fours making the whole scene much more frightening.

Ethan caught a quick glimpse of the face of one of his assailers and saw that he, too, wore a blindfold. He thought their lack of sight would be an advantage for him, so he made the first move, slashing down towards the face of his foe. The Watcher dodged the blow with uncanny precision.

"I can hear your blade foolish boy," shrieked the Watcher.

Ethan couldn't believe it but it gave him and idea: "Eisley, wave the lantern at them."

She picked up the lantern that lay between them on the ground and did as her brother instructed. This defensive attempt seemed to work much better than the first, for the two Watchers that had been crawling towards Eisley leapt backwards with a howl. Ethan took the lantern from Eisley and began to swing round in a circle drawing closer and closer to his retreating adversaries.

Meanwhile, Canis and Torolf were still locked in a battle of their own at the opposite end of the cove. Torolf was by far the bigger of the two, yet Canis was quicker. Canis tactfully dodged the heavy blows of his leader, throwing Torolf's balance and slowing him down. But often Torolf's fierce swats would connect with Canis and send him flailing against rocks.

Ethan held his own, pushing the Watchers toward the back wall of the encircling rocks. With each step the twins advanced closer to Canis' and Torolf's fight.

Miraculously, Canis had managed to pin Torolf to the ground pressing his face hard against the rocky surface. The Watchers heard their master's cry for help and ran to his aid, leaving Ethan and Eisley standing alone. Within moments the Hands of Smarr rent Canis from Torolf's back. They began to tear at him like predators hungry for their prey.

Torolf, now free from Canis, redirected his efforts on the Lambents. Ethan, fearing for Eisley's life tossed the lantern to her and shouted, "Don't let go of it!" He turned to face the monstrosity of a man, sword at the ready.

"You will not take us!" shouted Ethan.

Torolf seemed not to even notice Ethan. His mind was fixed upon the lantern dangling from Eisley's hand.

Ethan lunged towards Torolf and swung the sword at him. The enemy ducked and continued forward, pushing Ethan to the side like a play toy. Ethan chased after the Watcher, slashing at Torolf's legs. Torolf dodged Ethan's attempts.

Eisley backed toward the only exit in the cove. She was almost there when the other three Watchers suddenly dropped down between Eisley and her escape. They had left Canis for dead and came again to the aid of their leader.

Torolf bore down on Eisley. "Give me that lantern, girl!"

"No!" shouted Eisley. She shielded the lantern with her body, holding it behind her.

In one last desperate effort, Ethan jumped upon Torolf's back, trying to choke him from behind. Torolf wrenched Ethan over his shoulder and slung him at Eisley. The Lambents collided and the lantern's light was extinguished. Everything went dark and Ethan lay unconscious on the ground.

Calling out to her brother in the endless night, Eisley felt around for him. Finding Ethan she shook him, pleading for him to wake.

"The lantern, if you please?" growled Torolf. "Or you'll end up like your brother here!"

"No! You can't have it! I won't give it to you!" shouted Eisley, backing closer to the Watcher who blocked the way out. Without the light Eisley lost all sense of direction. The darkness pressed in upon her as if it had come to life.

"Very well," said Torolf. "If you will not part with the lantern then you will come with it!"

With those words Torolf snatched up Eisley like a rag doll. She held fast to the lightless lantern and Torolf took off into the everlasting night, followed by the other Hands of Smarr.

Chapter Twenty One
A Reason to Hope

Sometime later, Ethan woke in complete darkness and found that he had been left for dead in a sightless country that was not his own. He was alone, or thought he was. The last thing he remembered was Torolf throwing him at his sister. He called out to her but there was no response. Panic seized him. Where was Eisley? He fumbled around, grasping for her in the darkness.

"Eisley!"

Despair's stronghold grew with every breath. Then he heard something. Nearby, someone spoke softly.

"Hello! Who's there? Canis, is that you?"

Ethan made his way carefully toward the sound of the faint voice. He found Canis moments later. The Gloamer lay, face down, in an unnatural position as if he'd been twisted around. Ethan turned Canis over and a cry of anguish escaped from the Watcher. He was covered in a wetness that could only be blood.

"Eisley..." Canis could barely speak.

"I don't know where she is! She's not answering and it's your fault!" Ethan shook Canis violently.

Canis screamed again, but Ethan felt no remorse. It had been the Watcher's lies that led to this awful reality.

"She's been taken to Smarr," rasped Canis.

"What! No!"

"I…I will help you rescue your sister."

"How? *You* can't walk in your condition and *I* can't see."

"You will have to carry me. *I* will be your eyes and *you* will be my legs."

Ethan didn't like this plan. He wanted nothing more than to hear Canis breathe his last for what he'd done. But while his hatred for Canis was great, his love for Eisley was greater. Ethan agreed and lifted the injured man onto his back and they began their cumbersome journey toward The Rise, toward Smarr, and hopefully toward Eisley.

Every step seemed a danger to the now blind son of Glæm. He had no idea how they would possibly make it to Eisley.

"How am I supposed to get anywhere?" asked Ethan, frustrated by the uneven terrain that he was failing to traverse.

"You have to rely on your sense of hearing," answered Canis. "Stop for a second. Calm yourself."

Ethan did so.

"Now, listen…what do you hear?"

"Nothing! I hear nothing!"

"Calm. Listen closer," said Canis. "You will begin to hear the wind blowing lightly upon the surrounding rocks. You will hear our breathing and even the beating of our hearts. There are many things to hear."

Ethan quieted his mind and listened. He heard both his heartbeat and Canis', the latter of which wasn't beating in rhythm. Ethan knew this was a bad sign. Then Ethan began to hear… "The wind! I hear the wind!"

"Good," replied Canis. "Concentrate on the wind – that is what you'll use to get to your sister."

"Alright," said Ethan, unconvinced. "What now?"

"Move forward slowly and listen for the pattern of the wind to change," instructed the Gloamer.

Ethan did so and was surprised to find he could hear slight variations in the wind. He acknowledged this.

"Good. Now, when it sounds as if the wind has stopped you'll know you have reached an obstacle. Then use your feet to test the ground in front of you. If you don't hear a change in the wind's pattern, you can continue forward."

"How is this possible?" asked Ethan. "Why have I never been able to hear like this before?"

"When one has lost a sense, it gives more precision to the others," answered Canis. "When I first began to use my eyes I could no longer call on my sense of hearing in the same ways that I'd been accustomed to all my life."

"Is this how all Gloamers get around – by listening to the wind?" asked Ethan in bewilderment.

"No," replied Canis, "There are other ways, but there's no time now."

The two handicapped men carried on in this manner for hours, though, to Ethan, it felt like an eternity. Canis instructed and led Ethan when he could, but the Gloamer's life was waning. Ethan became accustomed to walking without sight, but the extra burden of carrying a dying man on his back kept their progress slow.

There came a point where Canis no longer spoke. Ethan could tell by his short breaths that he still lived, but for how long was uncertain. The fear of the unknown seized Ethan as he thought of the great open expanse that surely surrounded him. He thought of running into large creatures like the Squalor. If that wolf-like beast did come upon him, would he hear it? Would he smell it? The thought of cliffs and ravines caused his chest to tighten. Despair had nearly over taken him; he couldn't go on. The darkness was too much. Dropping to his knees, Ethan slid Canis off of his back. He lay down next to the Gloamer, utterly exhausted.

Trying to conquer his fear, he thought of Eisley. Those monsters had taken her to Smarr. What was Smarr? Was he a man like the Watchers had turned out to be? Or, was he something else? Eisley knew what he was, if she was even still alive. No! She had to be alive! Ethan got to his feet. But he couldn't go on carrying the dying Gloamer as he had. It was Canis's own fault wasn't it? He'd betrayed them and this was the payment. But, wasn't he dying because he had been trying to save Ethan and his sister's lives?

Ethan began to understand the terrible truth: that *he*, not the Gloamer, had been the cause of everything that had happened. He had decided to leave home. Eisley had followed him, not the Gloamer. Now Ethan felt true remorse for Canis. But he still couldn't carry him. Canis was too heavy and Ethan was too tired. Crying, Ethan bent low and told Canis that he'd forgiven him and apologized that he couldn't carry him any further. Canis did not answer. With a heart burdened by abandoning the Gloamer, Ethan headed off in the direction he'd been traveling – into the wind.

Not long after leaving Canis, the absurdity in what Ethan was trying to accomplish came crashing down on him. He was one person in the middle of a vast unknown land that was veiled in darkness. He was trying to get to the very cause of the darkness by himself, on foot, without the aid of his eyes. As hard as he tried, he couldn't keep these thoughts out of his mind. He felt that they were being put there by something; perhaps the darkness itself dealt these ideas. The pitch black was so tangible – the realest thing he'd ever known or experienced next to the light. How could the light have created this horrible darkness?

Ethan was in his most desperate hour, stumbling again and again over the rugged terrain beneath his feet. He crawled to keep from falling over, moving against the wind, but then the wind changed direction and threw him completely off course. He was lost in the darkness with no way of escape. Despair finally had his way with Ethan. He dropped to the ground and because there was no option left to him, Ethan called out for help. He called and he called but nothing happened. This was the end. He knew he would die alone in the darkness.

There in that wretched moment, when all hope was surely lost, he began to hallucinate. In the distance he thought he saw a small light. Blinking then wiping the sweat and grit from his eyes he tried to make the illusion go away. It didn't disappear but only grew more vivid. Now there was more than one light. There were four lights, and they were getting closer. Was he delirious? As the lights came nearer, it appeared that they weren't lights at all, but cloaked…glowing people. Yes, he'd completely lost his mind. Ethan reached out toward the four figures in desperation.

Chapter Twenty Two
Collision

The illusion grew clearer. The light became so brilliant that Ethan covered his eyes, ducking low to the ground in fear. He heard footsteps drawing near and he cowered even more. Suddenly the noise ceased and he was sure the hallucination had ended. But something turned him over and lifted him up to itself.

"Get away! Leave me alone!" yelled Ethan.

"Ethan? Ethan!" cried the voice.

The voice sounded familiar. He opened his eyes and there was his mother. Except it wasn't exactly as he remembered her because her face was glowing. She reminded him of the lantern. Then he recalled the story of how, in the darkness, Glæmians supposedly shone with the Light of Glæm.

"Mother?"

"Oh, Ethan! Yes its me!" said Evangeline with a tenderness that he'd missed so much. "We thought we'd lost you!"

Ethan clung to his mother. He began to cry and such joyous tears they were.

"But...how did you find me?

"By the Creator's hand." said his father, appearing and falling to his knees to hold tight to his son. "There's no other explanation."

Ethan held fast to his parents.

"We didn't know where to find you," said Amory. "But we were determined to search the world over until we did, my boy!"

"Eisley! She's been taken to...to Smarr," stuttered Ethan.

"We know, love," cried Evangeline. "We know."

"How?" asked Ethan.

"We found the Gloamer you were traveling with, and he told us."

"Canis is still alive?"

"Barely," replied Grandpa Emmett, walking up to Ethan's side. "Grandma is tendin' to him just over there," said the old man nodding toward Jaine, who knelt on the ground over a still body a few feet from the rest of the Lambents. "He's the reason we found ya."

"Grandpa!" shouted Ethan. "You and Grandma are here, too?"

Emmett bent down next to Amory and Evangeline with a look of defeat upon his face. "I'm sorry I let ya go alone, lad. I should've known better."

Emmett ran his hands through Ethan's hair. Ethan noticed his parents giving Emmett a scolding look that could only mean there had been hard feelings towards him for his actions.

"Its not your fault Grandpa, it's mine...it's mine," cried Ethan. "It's my fault that Eisley..."

"Now, now. You needn't worry 'bout that, boy," said Emmett. "We're goin' to get'er presently."

"The Gloamer told us how to get to The Rise," said Amory.

"Canis saved my life," said Ethan. "Twice."

"Well, then, we're indebted to him," replied his mother.

"We'll do everything we can to save him," said Grandma Jaine, who had come up from behind and kissed Ethan on the forehead. She too was glowing like the rest of his family.

Ethan lay in a state of disbelief. His family encircled him, looking down on him in complete love. He had never felt so safe in all his life. The feeling was more than he could have possibly hoped for. In his hopelessness he called out for help. And while he thought his cry had gone unnoticed he knew now that it most certainly had not .

"The Light," said Ethan.

"What dear?" asked Evangeline.

"How are you all glowing?"

"The Light of Glæm lives within us, son," answered his father. "You know this." Ethan had heard it his whole life, yet, only now did he see how true it really was.

"Why am I not glowing?" He seemed so dead in comparison to his family.

"You will in time…when you trust in the Light," answered Amory.

"But how could I not believe?" said Ethan, gazing upon his shining family. "I mean…look at all of you."

"There must be something deep within that still prevents you from truly believing," replied his mother. "You, yourself, must have faith in the Light. You cannot rely on our belief alone. It is a choice that you alone must make."

"We ought'a get goin'," growled Emmett, standing to his feet. "I've got a granddaughter to save!"

Side by side, the Lambent family crossed the dark country of Gloam, pulling Canis along on makeshift stretcher. It didn't seem quite as dark as it once had, and truthfully it *wasn't* as dark as it had been. The light exuding from the Lambents shone brightly into the night, pushing back doubt and despair. They left the rocky terrain where Ethan, Eisley and Canis had been attacked, and were now in the flat lands heading toward The mountain of Smarr.

Ethan, still weak from the fight and carrying Canis, rode on Amory's back. As they walked, Ethan recounted all that had happened to them since leaving the company of his grandfather. He told his family of Maridia and the discovery of Earnest Lambent traveling there. They were all surprised by this news but even more surprised by Earnest's journal, which Ethan still carried in his pack. He told them of Jukes, the Overseer of Maridia, and Delia, his daughter (while leaving out one small detail concerning a kiss). Then, with a great sadness he told his family of the twins' great protector: Deerborn and his wife, Abril. He recounted the story of the blacksmith, Mikael Temujin who had forged his and his sister's blades. He described their journey through the Deadwood where the Breath-of-Smarr had nearly pushed them back. Then, with a shutter, Ethan told the Lambents of his encounter with the *real* Squalor and of delivering the deathblow to the beast with his new sword (at this his mother gasped). He recounted his first battle with the Watchers, or the Hands of Smarr as they were rightfully called, and of the town of By Down. Lastly he recounted, in detail, the most recent encounter with the Watchers that brought Eisley's captivity.

In turn, Ethan's family told him of their journey across the northern parts of the Camel Back Mountains and of their meeting with the people of Farthenly, who, because of Jaine's heritage, gave them a guide that took them to the edge Gloam, through the very same Deadwood that the twins had traveled through. They had traveled far north of the path Ethan had taken. Then they told him of their encounters with the Hands of Smarr and how they fought them off several times, always succeeding because Smarr's servants were so afraid of the light within them.

"So they know you're here, too?" asked Ethan. "How many were there?"

"There were four," said Amory.

"That's how many we fought," said Ethan. "Besides Canis, who must have been the fifth one."

Ethan looked over at the unconscious Watcher being pulled by Emmett and wondered what would become of him.

As they traveled, Ethan wondered why he hadn't begun to glow yet. Obviously the Creator existed because the light was real and alive in his family. Yet, why did the darkness plague the world so? Why would the Light allow it? If these questions were answered then perhaps he'd finally understand. Perhaps all doubt would be cast away.

There came a point where, in the far distance, a great shadow began to loom on the edge of the horizon. If Gloam had been completely dark (as it had), then the great shadow in the distance was something even darker than darkness itself. Whatever they were approaching was enormous. Ethan suspected that it was The Rise, the dwelling place of Smarr. As they got closer to the shadow, this suspicion was proven true.

By the light within them, the Lambents saw the mountain. It was tall, too tall, in fact, to see its peak, which disappeared into the blackness above. Finally, Ethan and his family reached the mountain base and the men began to climb, leaving both Evangeline and Jaine at the bottom to look after Canis. Immediately Ethan realized that The Rise was exactly like the Camel Back Mountains, though void of vegetation like everything else in Gloam. He thought this to be a strange coincidence. It was as if this mountain had somehow gotten separated from the others when they'd all sprung up from the belly of the world. The only major difference was that The Rise appeared to be even larger than some of the mountains he'd crossed over in the Camel Back Range.

They reached a ceiling of thick, looming clouds and still the mountain continued upward. On the verge of pushing through the clouds, the Lambents were stopped dead in their tracks by none other than Torolf and his minions. They had with them two prisoners.

"Eisley! Deerborn!" shouted Ethan.

His sister and friend were bound together, gagged and blindfolded. They both fought hard against their captor, the largest of the Watchers, who held them both over one of his broad shoulders with irregular ease.

Eisley tried to screamed through the gag in her mouth.

"Let them go!" shouted Amory. "You have faced us before and you've fled each time. Do not continue to make the same mistake."

"Your trickery won't work this time Glæmian!" hissed the leader. Then holding up the lightless Magic Lantern he said, "I have recently come to realize that your lights can be extinguished." A hideous grin crossed his blindfolded face revealing razor sharp teeth.

"You might find *our* lights a bit harder to put out than that trinket yer carryin' there!" said Emmett, with a grin of his own.

"We shall see!" Torolf dove toward Emmett who mirrored the action. They clashed in midair, dropping to the ground in a knotted heap. Amory leapt toward the leader from behind, aiding his father. Both men struggled to keep their grip on Torolf as he thrashed about like a feral beast.

The largest Watcher backed away from the fight holding tight to his captives while the remaining two crawled forward to help their leader. Ethan ran to face them, drawing his sword and releasing a fierce war cry. The two enemies, perceiving Ethan's advance, moved to counter, but collided with one another. Ethan ducked out of the way and his blade met the stomach of one of the wild men who fell shrieking down the side of the mountain. As the injured Watcher fell away into the darkness below, the ground began to shake, sending all those left upon the mountainside tumbling after.

Chapter Twenty Three
Wake Up O' Sleeper

Within moments, Lambent and Watcher alike slammed into the flatlands below. The ground continued to shake. Ethan struggled to stand, trying to maintain his balance. In the commotion of the fall, Eisley and Deerborn had been separated from the Hands. Evangeline saw her daughter and rushed to her side. She called for Ethan to bring his sword to free Eisley. Ethan came to his mother's beckoning and cut the bindings on both Eisley and Deerborn. Eisley removed her blindfold and, upon seeing her mother, cried for joy and burst into light. She had immediately understood why her mother was glowing. Eisley had awoken! Ethan stood by, watching this transformation in awe. Yet *he* was still more like the darkness than the light.

Deerborn, now completely free of his bindings, came to Ethan and clasped his arm. "Thank you, young man." Ethan felt that, in that moment, Deerborn was accepting him as a comrade-at-arms, rather than a charge to protect. Then, in a flash, he was off to the aid of Amory and Emmett who had begun to fight the Watchers again.

With the ground still shaking, Eisley stumbled to Ethan and the twins embraced. Jubilation filled Ethan's heart at finding his sister alive. At same time he knew confusion and sorrow because he hadn't transformed like she.

Then, Ethan's roving eyes found the inanimate Watcher he'd stabbed lying close by. This made him eager to join his family in the fight. The remaining three Watchers surrounded Amory, Emmett and a sword-less Deerborn, who were all corralled back-to-back, parrying blows from the enemy. Ethan left his sister's side and ran to help his family, weapon in hand. Eisley and Evangeline went to Jaine and Eisley clung to her grandmother. Jaine was trying her best to protect Canis by lying low behind a boulder. Eisley saw the injured Gloamer and shouted his name in surprise.

Despite the commotion of battle, Torolf heard Eisley's raised voice.

"Canis still lives?" growled Torolf. He called to Rafe, the largest of their ranks, and ordered him to do away with the young traitor. Rafe left the encircled enemy and began sniffing out Canis and the Lambent women.

Meanwhile, Ethan approached the Watchers from the rear. Either Ethan had honestly gone unnoticed by the enemy or they were simply more interested in the foe they surrounded. Nevertheless, stealthily approaching the Watchers and realizing that his weapon would be of much more use to Deerborn, Ethan yelled to the soldier and tossed his sword over the heads of the Watchers. Deerborn caught the sword by the hilt and a look of immense satisfaction crossed his face. Deerborn began attacking the enemy with the precision of a fully trained swordsman. Then and there, the one Watcher remaining with Torolf fell at the hands of Deerborn.

After Deerborn felled the Watcher, Amory and Emmett were freed to chase after Rafe, who neared Canis and the women, leaving only Deerborn and Ethan to face the leader. Torolf was enraged at the death of his fallen comrade and fought with a new vigor. He grabbed Deerborn with an unparalleled strength, knocking the sword from the Maridian's hand. Ethan pulled at Torolf's legs, screaming at the Watcher to release Deerborn, who struggled under the girth of the evil Gloamer.

Rafe found the women. They had moved to surround Canis in a last ditch effort to save him. Eisley, in a moment of pure courage, snuck around the large Watcher and climbed the boulder they were using for cover. From that position she found the advantage. Eisley sailed from the rock onto the back of Rafe and held fast to the wriggling giant. Then, wrenching the blindfold free from his hairy face, Eisley exposed Rafe to the Light shinning through them. Amory and Emmett arrived at the scene and Emmett hollered, "That's my girl!"

Rafe was terrified. Howling, he fell to the ground to cover his exposed eyes.

The ground continued to shake.

Ethan and Deerborn struggled with Torolf who still held them at bay. Ethan noticed the Magic Lantern dangling from Torolf's belt and ran into the darkness scouring the ground for the sword that Deerborn had dropped. He couldn't explain it, but he felt that if he had the lantern, he could save them from the Watchers and possibly from Smarr.

He found his blade and ran back to the fight where he managed to cut the lantern free from Torolf's side. The Lambent heirloom hit the ground with a CLANG and rolled to a stop near Ethan's feet. This drew Torolf from his fight with Deerborn and he galloped toward Ethan, hissing and howling as he came. Ethan reached down and grabbed the lantern. Upon touching it, the Magic Lantern burst to life and a brilliant light stretched out from it then shot up into the clouds as it did on the day Ethan killed the Squalor. A moment later the light bolted from the lantern and disappeared over the horizon. To all the onlookers it appeared that the light had fled.

Abruptly, the earthquake ceased.

Then the mountain behind Ethan tore loose from the ground and sprang into the thick clouds above! Everyone turned in confusion, including Torolf and Rafe, the last of the Watchers. A massive hole gaped where a mountain had been only moments before. Abruptly, the Hands of Smarr began to convulse violently; both fell to the ground and started foaming at the mouth. No sooner had their fit begun than it ceased and the Watchers stood simultaneously, as if controlled by a puppet master. There they remained, still as statues until they began to speak in unison. It was not their voice, but a darker, ancient voice that came forth from their mouths – the voice of Smarr.

"Enough!" bellowed Evil.

The beating of massive wings was heard circling high above. The Lambents peered skyward, but could see nothing.

Without warning, a black mist-like substance shot from the clouds above, and, like a giant lasso, it pulled the *glowing* Lambents and Deerborn into a group while winding its way around them. Tighter and tighter became the dark bindings and, try as they might to escape, the captives were helpless to its power. Ethan remained outside the mist looking on in fear as it held his family together.

As the mist grew around his family, it became harder to see them and then he understood why he hadn't been pulled in. Whatever created the mist wanted to hide the light of his family from itself. But why had Deerborn been bound with them? The Maridian was like Ethan – lightless.

Something hit the ground so hard, it brought Ethan to his knees. The Watchers hadn't fallen; they remained like stone for a moment moving, suddenly, towards Ethan. He got back to his feet and backed away running into an unexpected barrier that hadn't been there before. Slowly he turned.

Before him was a creature larger than life, as large as a mountain in fact. He knew, then and there, that The Rise was not actually a mountain at all, but the vile creature Smarr to whom all this darkness was attributed.

The monster's face dropped directly in front of Ethan. Smarr's body appeared to be made of large semi-transparent plates of rock that shifted back and forth as it sniffed at the Glæmian boy. Its eyes were ancient and as glossy as polished black marble. In them Ethan saw his own reflection and felt as if he'd seen the state of his own heart: dark and devoid of any real substance. He stood mesmerized by his own thoughts, or were they his own thoughts? He couldn't be sure.

"There is no light, all that I need is found in the darkness," he said aloud to himself, still peering into the fathomless depths of the giant eyes.

"I can become one with the dark and never want for anything again," he continued.

"I am nothing, unless...I become one with you," said Ethan, to Smarr.

"I cannot be satisfied without you," said the young helpless Glæmian.

"You are nothing unless you become one with me," came the deep voice of Smarr through the Watchers who moved in directly behind Ethan.

Hearing the words from Torolf and Rafe, Eisley shouted to her brother. "No, Ethan! Don't listen to him. You are my brother. You are a son of Glæm and descendent of the Boy of Legend – Riley Lambent!" At the mention of Riley, Smarr stomped the ground and the Watchers hissed. "You don't belong to this filth! Look at me! Look to the Light!"

Ethan stood motionless, not sure of the stranger's voice that called out to him in the distance. He knew he recognized it and yet nothing seemed more familiar to him now than his own reflection in the eyes of the archaic creature standing before him.

"Remember the lantern!" cried Eisley from the other side of the mist.

"The lantern?" thought Ethan. He did remember a lantern. It had been with him through most of his journey and had kept him from being fully enveloped in the darkness – the cold darkness that now took him. Oh, how the light was so much warmer and safer than what he felt now. He remembered the light and it grew in his mind and heart.

"NO!!" screamed Smarr, reading Ethan's thoughts.

The terror in that demanding voice jarred Ethan to his senses, and for the first time in his life everything began to make perfect sense. Ethan truly understood the darkness, while staring into its horrifying face. If Light, the Creator, was perfect, then nothing else could be perfect or else it too would be the Creator. Then Ethan's head cleared completely as Smarr was driven utterly from his mind and the answer to his most troubling question was revealed to him. If the Light was perfection and everything that was good, then the darkness was all that was flawed and bad. At the core of the imperfection was this loathsome creature Smarr. Not only was the darkness imperfect, but so was the world – Gloam, The Camel Back Mountains, even Glæm. The only truly flawless thing was the brilliant Light that lived in his family and which had been in the lantern moments ago – the Light of the Creator.

Something began to happen within Ethan. Warmth bubbled up from his core and· stretched outward, slowly filling his whole body. The sensation made its way up Ethan's throat and into his head, filling him with the most wonderful feeling that he'd ever experienced. Then a most delightful thing happened. Though standing face to face with Evil, Ethan began to laugh aloud! A laughter of pure joy. Light erupted from him, brighter than any Glæmian had ever seen. The light spilt out of him and into the face of darkness.

The Watchers screamed and fell convulsing to the ground.

The giant monster launched into the sky, beating his massive wings, flying higher and higher into the dark clouds above. The wind of the wings knocked Ethan off of his feet. The Watchers continued to voice Smarr's anger, the black mist surrounding the Lambents dissipated, and they, along with a bewildered Deerborn, ran to Ethan's side. In the midst of all this dread, the most wonderful thing had happened. Ethan truly believed in the Light.

The celebration was short lived, however. From the mouths of the Watchers came the words, "RUIN, DISFIGURE, BLIGHT AND MAR! INJURE, MAIM, DESTROY AND SCAR!"

High above, the Lambents saw the mountainous evil descending towards them. As he dove landward, the darkness in his eyes created a vacuum that began to pull at the light within the Lambents.

The Lambent family cried out at the soul-wrenching pain. They had never felt such excruciating torment and none thought they would survive it. The light was being pulled from them, as if their very essence was being extinguished. When the Lambents were certain of death, the light that had exited the lantern minutes earlier reappeared. It came racing back from the west and settled into the lantern. Smarr's attack ceased as another explosion of light shot out of the lantern. The Lambents stopped screaming as the pain subsided, while the Watchers, having felt the explosion of light, yelped with tortured howls. Then from the west came dozens of behemoth lights flying through the clouds above. The lights ate away the dark clouds as they came. They began to circle in the deteriorating clouds just above the Lambents, and above Smarr. As they drew closer, spiraling down, Ethan saw clearly that they were just like Smarr, except brilliantly lit. He couldn't completely make out their shapes because light exuded from the core of the creatures, shining completely through their glassy surfaces.

Smarr attempted to get away, but within moments the bright creatures had completely surrounded him. The Lambent family could no longer make out what was happening. The ground rumbled and it sounded as if the new creatures began to sing or chime, spinning so fast now that all that could be seen was a large solid stream of light. Abruptly, it was all over. All but one of the creatures flew off in the westward direction from where they came.

The Lambents saw Smarr in the distance as he *had* been: a mountain. He appeared lifeless. It was clear that the one remaining creature of light, like Smarr, had been a mountain as well. Certainly it had come from Camel Back Mountains Range. Now Ethan's idea of the mountains being like giant sleeping turtles seemed probable.

The being of light flew close to the Lambents and then spoke within the Glæmians. "Smarr knew the time would come when the heirs of Riley Lambent would return to this land to bind him. He knew and he feared your return with every beat of his wretched heart. For now, the Ancients have bound Smarr to the earth, but only for a short time. He is much stronger than we are."

"If you can't stop Smarr, then how can he be defeated?" asked Ethan, confounded by the thought of Smarr being stronger than the combined power of these Ancients. "Greater is the Light that is within you than the darkness that is within the world," said the Ancient. "Soon you will be called upon to harness the power of the Light and put an end to Smarr thereby destroying all he has caused by his arrogance."

"How long will he remain bound?" asked Amory.

The Ancient did not answer Amory's question, but rather said, "As it is written, 'They took the lantern forged by the Seer to the top of the wretched being, Smarr, and they undid all that he had done to the dark land.' I will await your return and when you are ready I will take you home."

The Lambents did not understand what the Ancient had meant by, 'as it is written' or 'the lantern forged by the Seer' but they had only one lantern with them – the Magic Lantern. So with those instructions, the Lambent family wasted no time scaling the back of the dormant evil, crossing into what remained of the cloud-bank and reaching the summit. Deerborn stayed with the Ancient and Canis, who remained unconscious.

Together, on the top of Smarr, Ethan and Eisley, held high the Magic Lantern, surrounded by their family. The light from within the lantern shot out far and wide causing the skies of Gloam to grow clear. In the lesser light of the night, Gloamers saw the moons and stars in the heavens above for the first time. And there on the back of that darkest evil, the reunited Glæmians stood together and watched the sun rise on the land of Gloam for the first time in millennia.

To be continued in

STIRRING

BOOK TWO OF THE EMBLEM AND THE LANTERN

A note from the author:

So many questions are left unanswered! What are the Ancients and who is the Seer that they spoke of? What will become of Gloam and its inhabitants now that the darkness has disappeared? How long will the vile creature Smarr be subdued? What of the puzzling emblem that Ethan dreamt of? Do the Lambents and their magical family heirloom have a larger role to play in the coming events?

Join Ethan and Eisley Lambent as they begin to uncover the answers to these mysteries and many others in *Stirring - Book Two of The Emblem and The Lantern* coming soon!

Further up and further in,
Dylan Higgins

ABOUT THE AUTHOR

Dylan Higgins is a husband, father, son, brother, friend, pastor, worship leader, teacher, student, storyteller, singer / songwriter, graphic designer and a lover of life, in general.

Dylan and his family reside in Brooks, Georgia in a home they've named *Spalding's End*, having been built many decades ago on the edge of a county bearing the same name. As it happens, Dylan's wife grew up in this very home just as their children are currently doing.

ABOUT THE ILLUSTRATOR

Mikael Jury is a student at Belhaven University in Mississippi. In addition to being an illustrator, Mikael is a fine blacksmith who is currently forging the Magic Lantern in his smithy. Mikael and Dylan are a part of the same church community, which is where their legendary partnership in this series first began!

ACKNOWLEDGEMENT

My deepest gratitude to all of the following. This adventure wouldn't have been nearly as amazing without each and every one of you! My wonderful wife, JoAlison who first believed in my abilities to write and who, furthermore, feared for the lives of our children through the pages of this book. It's not really them babe! My children, Ethan and Eisley who are wonderful and inspirational enough to inspire an entire series of books! I pray that your real-life journey will outshine the characters of this book. Mikael Jury who has journeyed along side me from the beginning of this project bringing key scenes to life through your unique illustrations. Further up and further in Mikael! Susan Clough for editing the first edition. Joanna Jury for rising to the challenge of editing the new edition - it trills me to have you on this journey! To those of you who read the majority of Awakening as I was drafting it: Jo, Mom, Josh Campbell and Joanna Jury. Thank you all for your honest critique and ideas. Clay Parker who brought certain aspects of the story to life through film. You, my friend, are truly a visionary! I can't wait for the movie! Mike Sherrard who first dreamed, with me, of story about a magical lantern. Professor D. Scott Henderson, Ph.D who continues to be a formative influence in my study of philosophy. Your teaching can, consequently, be seen through certain subject matter herein. Elizabeth Lipham who took a rough theme song and smoothed it out in amazing ways with your violin playing and singing! To the Sleepy Turtles who helped to bring the soundtrack of Awakening to life! I look forward to more musical adventures with you! To everyone who has supported me through *Awakening's* first year of life. To all who has read or will read this story - I hope it inspires you to do amazing things! To Christ our Lord who has given mankind the ability to dream. Our art is simply a replica of Yours' and everything we imagine is only possible because You have first imagined it. You are perfection!

Made in the USA
Columbia, SC
08 August 2019